W9-CEC-755

The Life *before* Her Eyes

Also by Laura Kasischke

NOVELS

Suspicious River

White Bird in a Blizzard

POETRY COLLECTIONS

Wild Brides

Housekeeping in a Dream

Fire & Flower

THE LIFE *before* HER EYES

LAURA KASISCHKE

HARCOURT, INC.
New York San Diego London

www.HarcourtBooks.com

Library of Congress Cataloging-in-Publication Data
Kasischke, Laura, 1961–
The life before her eyes/Laura Kasischke.—1st ed.
p. cm.
ISBN 0-15-100888-4
1. Teenage girls—Fiction. 2. Choice (Psychology)—Fiction.
3. Female friendship—Fiction. 4. Murderers—Fiction. I. Title.
PS3561.A6993 L54 2002
813'.54—dc21 2001024311

Text set in Garamond MT
Display set in Garamond MT and AGaramond
Designed by Cathy Riggs

First edition
A C E G I K J H F D B

Printed in the United States of America

For Bill

Voici que vient l'été, la saison violente
Et ma jeunesse est morte ainsi que le printemps

Summer is coming, the violent season
And my youth, dead with the spring

—APOLLINAIRE

Prologue

April

They're in the girls' room when they hear the first *dot-dot-dot* of semi-automatic gunfire. It sounds phony and far away, and they keep doing what they're doing—brushing their hair, looking at their reflections in the mirror...

Dot-dot-dot.

The mirror is narrow and institutional, but also brilliant. Earlier that morning, the janitor wiped it with Windex and a cloth, and now it's like a piece of mind there, opening. Clean as a thought in the mind of a god. A thought cast by the creator of everything onto perfectly calm water.

They have to stand shoulder to shoulder to squeeze both of their reflections in:

The dark-haired girl, smiling, her arm hooked into the arm of her friend.

The blond, who's been crying, but who's laughing now. Still, the crying's made a blurred photograph of her face—her mascara smeared, her image occurring to her as though from the surface of a shimmering pool.

"I'm just so happy for you," she says to her friend's reflection.

"Then why are you crying?" her friend asks. She laughs.

"Because I'm happy!"

"Are you sure you're not jealous?" the dark-haired girl asks, passing the hairbrush to her friend.

Dot-dot-dot.

Dot. Dot. Dot.

"What is that?"

The blond stuffs her hairbrush, which is now spun with gold and black silk (a miniature angel's nest) back into her backpack next to her anthology of English literature. The pages of that anthology are so thin, they're like dead girls' dreams, translucent skin. On them it seems that everything that has ever been thought has been written.

Knock-knock-knock-knock-knock.

This time it's followed by a soft and gurgling scream. The scream of someone slipping suddenly into a warm bath.

"Shit," one of the girls says.

"What the hell—"

One of the girls starts toward the door, but the other grabs her elbow. "Don't go," she says. "What if?—"

"What?"

"I don't know." She drops her friend's elbow.

"It's just a prank. It's probably Ryan Asswipe..."

Dot. Dot—

So loud this time—close and mechanically bright—that both girls scream. Their screams are followed by a silence that sounds foolish, cold and hard as the tile on the girls'-room walls. One says in a whisper, "It's Michael Patrick. Yesterday, in trig, he told me he was going to bring a gun to school, that he was going to kill..."

"Who? Kill who?"

"Everybody."

"What?"

"'All you fuckheads,' he said. I thought he was joking, you know what a freak—"

"Why didn't you tell anybody?"

"I—"

On the other side of the door to the girls' room, there's another scream. It sounds desperate and pointless as music, and it's followed by a man asking for help.

"Help," is all he says.

Mr. McCleod?

Then silence, except that one of the girls is wearing seven silver bangles on her right wrist, and both girls gasp when they jangle. The other grabs the bangles on her friend's wrist and holds them still with her hand.

Then he opens the door slowly, and steps in. He's holding a big blue-black gun with both hands, pointing it in front of him, aiming at nothing.

When he sees them, Michael Patrick laughs. "Hey," he says.

One of the girls, trying not to sob, swallows, then says, "Michael."

He's wearing a shiny shirt—a clean and pale white shirt, but there are large ugly sweat stains under his arms. There's an angry rash under his chin, where he must have shaved too fast that morning.

Michael Patrick smiles. He's breathing hard. He takes one of his hands off the grip of the gun and puts the hand in the pocket of his jeans. He's wearing white shoes with blue lightning bolts on the sides, laces untied.

"So," he says too loudly in the quiet softness of the girls' room, and both girls flinch.

"So," he says more softly, as if sorry to have startled them. "Which one of you girls should I kill?"

Neither girl breathes.

Both of them look at his face as if for the first time. What is he, standing in the girls' room with a gun? How many times have they passed Michael Patrick in the hall and never looked at him? A hatred moving among them, waiting. An ugliness, a nothing—a solid hole of it, swallowing.

Then he points the gun at one of them and then at the other and shouts, "Which one of you girls should I kill?!"

This time they don't flinch. Behind him there's still the mirror . . . a bit of infinity, which in its disinterest still holds their reflections safely in it.

One of the girls swallows, takes a deep breath. "Please," she whispers, "don't kill either of us."

Michael Patrick smirks, then says, "Oh, but I'm going to kill one of you, so which one should it be?"

He holds the gun closer to their faces, and they can smell it. Sulfur, oil.

The dark-haired girl clears her throat and says clearly, as if she'd been ready to say it for years, "If you're going to kill one of us, kill me."

Michael Patrick nods at her and smiles. He isn't in a hurry now, if he ever was.

"Well?" he says to the other girl. To the other girl he says, "What do you have to say?"

The blond sees her own face in the mirror behind him, feels the heat of her friend beside her, moist, alive, and she shifts her weight away. She looks down. Her friend is breathing calmly now. There are tears on the gray linoleum, and strange specks of gold among them, as if someone has ground jewelry into the floor with the heel of a shoe.

She closes her eyes.

The girls' room is sacred and full of waiting.

There is no one in it but the three of them. No one beyond it, either, it seems. No flag snapping in the breeze at the top of the flagpole outside. No bike rack glinting in the sun. No orange double doors, open or closed. No glass case full of golden trophies in the hall. No gym, shined up and smelling like rubber. No principal's office. No principal's desk cluttered with framed photos of confused-looking children and wives who are all different and all the same—young and beautiful and smiling, middle-aged and overweight—staring blankly out of the same, changed face.

No principal. No venetian blinds casting slatted shadows across his face.

No students standing with their backs against the brick walls, watching.

No vending machines purring in the cafeteria, and no elderly woman cutting Jell-O into emerald squares behind the chilled cafeteria glass, laying them trembling onto little white dishes.

There's no one out there. Not a janitor, not a secretary, not a soul, not God.

No one is going to hear what she says, whether she speaks or not. Simply, she could close her eyes and never speak again. She could suck all of the air in this room—every dust mote, every atom—into her body and hide it inside her. . . .

She is about to do it, about to inhale, when the silver bangles on her wrist make a tinny, unholy sound.

Her friend's grasp on them has slipped with trembling and sweat . . . the silver bracelets she bought at a boutique downtown last summer and which she'd slipped over her own thin and miraculous hand that very morning a million years ago.

Now that they are free of the other girl's grasp, they will not stop jangling.

They are cheap bells on the doors of convenience stores. They are small bells worn around the necks of cats. They are brass bells on reception desks . . . RING BELL FOR HELP. They are Salvation Army Santas' bells . . . the smell of gasoline in the grocery store parking lot, a handful of quarters dropped into a bucket, her own breath pouring out of her in the snowy cold, like a living scarf.

And beyond the distant sound of all the bells she's ever heard and loved, she can hear the sound of her own heart thumping dully inside her, pumping blood through her body, and she loves it, too . . . has always loved it, whether she knew it until now or not . . . loves it so much she would stay right here, like this, right here in this bathroom stall, terrified and violently alive for the rest of her life . . . an armful of silver bracelets, a rose tattooed on her hip—a bit of fatal beauty sewn directly into her skin—gold in her hair, a blush made of blooming and blood on her cheeks. She has crooked teeth, but it is her best flaw. She simply smiles with her mouth closed, and it makes her more mysterious. She would smile like that, beautifully, for the rest of her life if she could.

If she could.

But then Michael Patrick puts the gun near her ear. It touches her temple, and its blue blackness is a terrible, intimate whisper. . . .

She has to whisper back to it.

"Don't kill me," she whispers to it.

And when he asks, "Then who should I kill?"

She hears herself answer, "Kill her. Not me."

Part One

Sunlight

It was another beautiful day in a perfect life:

June again, and all the brilliance that came with it. All the soft edges of spring were gone, and a kind of clarity had taken their place. There was a sharpness to the trees and leaves, which were the green of bottle glass, while the sky beyond them had hardened into a pure and cloudless blue.

Diana McFee opened her eyes, and she might as well have been seeing the sky for the first time. Such a mundane surprise to be alive! A forty-year-old woman in the middle of June, looking straight into a very blue sky, a sky that looked like the center of something entirely fresh that had been neatly sliced in half with a sharp knife. A mind full of ether. A breathtaking emptiness, like a clean kitchen, a clear conscience.

She realized that she'd drifted into sleep while idling in the minivan, waiting for her daughter outside the elementary school, and had been startled awake by the hysteria of bells within the school's walls, up there on the hill, where the school day had just ended.

Inside, Diana knew, the girls were grabbing their jackets, pulling up their kneesocks, lining up outside the orange double doors that would burst open like a can of confetti in a moment. The green hillside would become a chaos of windbreakers and pigtails and the terrible bird shrieks of little girls.

But she was still in the process of waking, of rematerializing after her brilliant dream . . . a soccer mom stepping out of sleep as if it were a mirror, her body and mind coming together again atom by atom in the brightness where she waited.

She rubbed her eyes and inhaled.

Summer.

She loved summer. The way it dried and tidied everything up. All through March, April, May, Diana had been waiting for the struggle to be over—the smell of rotting and newness, the grass and the roots like damp hair. So much moisture involved in resurrection! The dirty puddles full of worms. The moist privacy of turtles scrambling out of the muck. All that birthing and blood, and the blatant sexuality of it. The teenage girls, too flushed, looking as if they'd just been dragged out of the mud by their hair.

In May, Diana could hardly stand to look at those teenage girls wearing their first short skirts and tank tops of the season after so much winter whiteness . . . those teenage girls waiting for the bus, crossing the street. The skin on their limbs looked barer than bare skin, as if the top layer of it had been peeled away, exposing to the air something more tender than flesh.

Winter lasted a long time in the Midwest. For five months those girls had been buried in snow.

But by mid-June they were wearing human skin again.

Diana loved June.

She realized again how much she loved it, as she unrolled the driver's side window of the minivan and breathed in the glassy air of it, knowing how much she loved it . . . all of it:

Summer, and her life . . . loved it with a heart that might as well have been made of tissue paper, it fluttered so lightly in her chest. There was the taste of pure sugar in her mouth. What had she last eaten? A peppermint? A sugar cube? Whatever it had been, it had been white and sweet, and she craved another.

She loved the sun on the side of her face, the smell of warm vinyl filling the minivan. She loved being herself in her forty-year-old body . . . being a wife, a mother . . . the bake sales and the field trips; the Band-Aids and the small sweaters coming out of the washer soggy and smelling of rain; the flour blended into butter and brown sugar, and the chocolate chips folded into that.

Now as she thought of it she realized that she loved *all* the material details of her days. The rolling heft of her silver minivan, the way the air parted to let it pass like a bullet on its way to the grocery store, the library, her child's elementary school, her part-time job.

She loved the sparkling clapboard house in which she lived on one of the nicest, shadiest streets—Maiden Lane!—in one of the most picturesque little college towns in the country.

Her daughter was pretty and happy.

Her husband was sexy, attentive, successful.

The world was very round. Round like a fishbowl. Thought swam around in circles in it.

How could they have ever believed it was flat? So much slipping and bending and arcing into space. Even at that moment, still stepping from her dream, Diana McFee could feel the roundness and hear the wind whispering as the earth turned in its grasp.

We are afloat in the sky, she thought, cradled, buoyed...

Mr. McCleod—a sad, short man with yellow teeth—looks up from the lesson he's trying to teach...

He almost never looks up. He is a painfully shy man, who makes teaching look like torture. His classroom is full of props that he can hide behind. Magnifying glasses. A television monitor. Computers. Microscopes. A transparency projector. And a map of the world beside a map of the human body—all its muscle groups and major organs labeled. Even the face on that human map looks like meat. And a skeleton, a real skeleton, which hangs from the wall at the front of the room... a skeleton with whom Mr. McCleod is rumored, jokingly, to be in love.

"She's a teenager," he told them on the first day of class in September.

He pointed out the narrowness of the pelvic bones and showed them how some of the bones that an older female skeleton would have were missing on this one. He explained there were bones in the female body that didn't ossify—*ossify: "to convert into bone,"* he wrote on the board in his lurching scrawl—until the human female was out of her teens.

Femoral bones, spinal vertebrae.

Those bones stayed soft inside the body for a long time, and if the girl died young, they simply melted away with her flesh.

Teeth and bones, Mr. McCleod told the class, would identify

them—who they'd been, what they'd done—long after they were dead. . . .

HER HUSBAND? HAD SHE BEEN THINKING OF HIM? Counting her many blessings?

Sexy, attentive, successful.

He was a respected professor of philosophy at the university. She'd been—the old story—his student.

And Diana herself was successful, though in a more modest sense than her husband. She was an artist—a sketch artist—and taught a few afternoons a week at the local community college. She spent her mornings in the studio her husband had finished for her above their garage, and drew. Pen and ink, graphite pencil, charcoal. Her work was sometimes used on the covers of poetry collections, literary magazines, church programs, calendars. She worked strictly in black and white... shadow and light.

And she was attractive. Still blond, though now she used a rinse to resuscitate the blond of her younger years. She was fit and slender, long-legged and blue-eyed as ever. She'd been told rather often that she resembled Michelle Pfeiffer, the Michelle Pfeiffer of the late 1990s, the one Diana used to watch on the movie channel, wishing (in vain, she'd assumed then) that she would look that good when she was almost forty.

And now she did.

Not that appearances were all that important to her now. She had wasted so much time in her teens primping, piercing, dieting... and that terrible tattoo, the rose they'd promised her wouldn't hurt but that nearly killed her as they sewed it into her skin, a permanent purple heart earned for naïveté in the face of a fad. She'd be buried, an old lady in a housedress, with that sexy teenage rose still blushing on her hip. Sometimes the thought of that made her sad; sometimes it made her laugh.

She didn't worry much about her appearance anymore... just enough to stay fit and wash her hair with Forever Blond once a week.

She wore simple clothing. She liked silks and Asian prints, dangling earrings and bangles. Today she was wearing a pair of shiny black slacks and a turquoise blouse. The blouse was sheer, but she wore a black tank top under it. A thin silver chain around her neck. An armful of silver bangles that made music as she walked, steered, brushed her hair.

Flat black shoes.

She dressed her age and income level, but did it creatively... a little exotic, like the artist underneath the soccer mom she was. She was, it always surprised her to be reminded, still sexy enough to be whistled at on occasion while crossing the street at a busy intersection. She hadn't expected that at forty. It was one of the many pleasant surprises of middle age.

She glanced at herself in the rearview mirror.

Her teeth were crooked, but her lips were pretty. She looked like the woman she'd wanted to be. *Someday this will be your life,* she used to think when she was a dreamy adolescent staring out the kitchen window of the apartment she shared with her divorced mother, fantasizing. *Someday this will be your life,* she thought to herself even now, as if it weren't, hearing her voice clearly in her own mind... the voice of the woman she had become, the pretty mother licking lipstick off her front teeth, smiling politely at her own reflection.

Summer...

And all the longing and damp hope of spring had finally

amounted to something. At home the peonies had ruffled up in the front yard like the sleeves of a fancy blouse—but sticky, sweet, crawling with little red ants.

The grass was green as eye shadow, green as satin.

The sky was a piece of hard candy.

And the bees hovered around the honeysuckle like tiny golden angels playing trumpets.

The lilies had just begun to open, and a breeze made out of perfume was passing from the pure centers of them into the world.

Mr. McCleod is reading aloud from the textbook. . . .

He is fiddling with his glasses as he reads, and his hands tremble.

Nicotine.

Perhaps he's thinking of nicotine as he reads to the class about one-celled organisms becoming two.

He hears the laughter of girls and looks up.

From the opposite sides of the classroom, they've caught each other's eyes.

They weren't trying to look at each other—they know better than that, know it will lead to uncontrollable laughter if their eyes meet across the room. But laughter is a vibrating wire strung between them. All they can do is avoid looking at one another, to keep from laughing. But as Mr. McCleod is reading, their eyes wander intuitively in the direction of Nate Witt—

Nate Witt.

The boy with the unfortunate name.

Nit wit.

The boy with the flat-green eyes.

There are miles and miles of AstroTurf reflected in those eyes.

He has a mean laugh and a habit of wiping his mouth with the back of his hand as if he's been boxing, as if he's just taken a punch to the jaw. He wears T-shirts with the names of bands and of baseball teams, faded jeans, and a pair of hiking boots every day. He's lean, with light brown hair, and neither girl has ever seen him laugh out loud, though they've seen him smile and smirk.

Nate Witt sits slumped and oblivious in the center of the room . . . stoned and openmouthed between them, and while they are trying to catch a glimpse of him from opposite ends of the biology classroom, they catch a glimpse of one another glimpsing at him and begin to laugh.

"Is there a problem, girls?" Mr. McCleod asks.

Both girls try to go expressionless, and shrug.

"No," one of them says, though her eyes are wide and wet and she has to bite her lips.

"No problem," the other says, raising her shoulders and letting them drop.

There's laughter sliding all around her like an electric dress.

Mr. McCleod puts his face back in his book and continues to read.

BACK HOME . . . THE HONEYSUCKLE. SHE HAD A LOVELY little garden waiting for her behind the house. A set of silver wind chimes dangling from a drainpipe under the eaves of the garage. In the breeze the wind chimes sounded like music made out of little girls' dreams . . . charm bracelets, porcelain dolls, the kind of teacups so delicate and thin that if you held them to the light you could see through them.

Whispers

At exactly 2:30 Diana glanced at her watch.

In five minutes they'd open the doors of her daughter's elementary school and let the little girls scamper back into the world. Deep at the center of herself she could feel the engine that kept her minivan idling. It purred on every side of her and over and under her... a great humming motor at the heart of her small universe. She was afraid she'd fall back to sleep, so she turned on the radio.

It was only static at first. *The whispers of the dead,* she thought in a flash, not knowing why she thought it. And then she adjusted the dial until she heard the voice of her favorite talk-show shrink.

"Of course she means it!" Dr. Laura said. "Drunks always *mean* they're going to quit."

"So... you think I need to see what she actually *does*?" the caller asked.

"Exactly. And don't count on anything. Thank you for your call."

There was a second of silence, the click of the caller being disconnected, and then Dr. Laura addressed the radio audience.

"Don't call me," she said, "and ask me whether your spouse is going to quit drinking. How should I know? I'm not God. Ask your spouse, and then—and this is the most important thing—ask yourself."

Diana felt a wisp of something—a little white feather, the kind stuffed deep inside a decorative pillow—brush her face with smug relief. Her husband didn't drink—or philander or gamble or take drugs. Never in seventeen years of married life had she felt the urge to ask anyone, especially not someone on the radio, for even the smallest scrap of advice.

"Hello, you're on the air," Dr. Laura said.

Again, a second of dead silence.

"Hel-lo? Are you there?"

"Ma'am?"

The caller was either an older boy or a woman with a very deep voice—a voice that sounded as if it were coming from the end of a long tunnel, a tunnel made of porous stone or cement, something that soaked up sound.

"Y-hes?" Dr. Laura said in a singsong that indicated impatience. "How can I help you?"

"I... I don't need help."

The voice was not hollow or breathy, but neither did it seem physical. The voice sounded like a recording of a recording played back at a too-slow speed.

"Well, then," Dr. Laura said, "why are you calling my show?"

There was a low grinding. Again the sound of a cassette tape played backward or too loosely, followed by machine grinding, and then the voice, faster and unnaturally bright, said, "I am in hell."

Diana exhaled as if she'd been punched, and she put her hand to her chest.

She looked up toward the hill, but the girls were still inside the school. Where were the other mothers? There was no one in the semicircular drive except herself...

Winter turns to spring, and everything melts.

The water in the drinking fountain in the high school hallway is nauseatingly warm, like human fluids.

Ryan Haslip puts his sister's bikini on Mr. McCleod's skeleton, and Mr. McCleod seems amused.

They have never seen him amused.

Someone puts a rose between the skeleton's bared teeth, and, along with the bikini, Mr. McCleod lets it stay.

IT COULD HAVE MEANT ANYTHING, BUT DIANA MCFEE felt a bright flash at the side of her face as if she'd been slapped fast by a cold hand, and she snapped the radio off.

She inhaled after what seemed like a long time and smelled something familiar but out of place in the air... the smell of the baking-supplies aisle at the grocery store. Spices, flour, crushed dry leaves.

I am in hell.

It could have meant, *I'm in love with a married man. My husband's cheating on me. I'm a shoplifter, a heroin addict, a pathological liar... guilty conscience, physical pain, mental illness, spiritual crisis. I'm in hell.*

What difference did it make? Whatever it was, she didn't want to hear it.

Maybe, she thought to herself, maybe she was tired of the radio altogether... these bodiless complaints traveling on the breeze, over lakes and playgrounds and cemeteries, to ask for help from strangers. So many souls in pain. They were all in hell, Diana thought, except that...

"Mommy?"

Diana hadn't seen her come out of the double doors or run down the green hill, but there her daughter was beside her in the front seat, looking prettily fresh, out of breath, utterly innocent.

"What's wrong, Mommy?" Emma asked.

Her eyes were pale blue and wide. Diana could see herself in them, looking twenty years younger than she was. No wrinkles in those little pools, no laugh lines. Just two tiny watery faces that had once belonged to her.

Diana looked away, shifted into reverse, glanced behind her in the rearview mirror.

"Nothing," Diana said. "You just scared me, that's all."

Emma said nothing. She looked at her own bare knees.

Diana pulled into the street, trying to drive slowly, but the two tons of steel and upholstery she was maneuvering out of the school's circular drive seemed only vaguely under her control. She'd never been a good driver, though she'd also never had an accident. Only terrible caution accounted for that. Back when she was a teenager, when she should have been learning to drive, she wasn't allowed to take driver's ed, because the semester it was offered she'd been caught with a Baggie of marijuana in her purse at school.

It was a red suede purse with a bit of fringe, and when her homeroom teacher, Mrs. Mueler, made her open it so she could look inside, it held the Baggie of marijuana, two tampons, a condom, a pack of matches, and a little billfold with a twenty in it.

Mrs. Mueler had smelled pot on her—that sweet weediness that lingered in Diana's long hair. She was fed up with girls like Diana, who was sent to the principal's office, but that wasn't enough for Mrs. Mueler. She demanded a list of restrictions, and driver's ed was one of them.

Finally it had been Diana's best friend, Maureen, who'd taught her to drive. Maureen had an old Honda Civic her father had given to her, and Maureen let Diana drive it around and around in circles in the mall parking lot on Sunday nights in the summer. Diana was just getting the hang of driving when—

"Shit!" she gasped, and slammed on the brakes and the horn at the same time.

She'd come within inches of the bumper of the minivan in front of hers, which had stopped suddenly to avoid hitting a little girl who'd dashed into the drive.

CHOOSE LIFE, a sticker on the bumper said.

"Jesus Christ!" Diana shouted.

"Mommy," Emma said. There was no judgment in it, just surprise.

Diana looked at her daughter.

Emma. Briefly, she'd forgotten. Emma's face was a parody of a pretty girl's, shocked. Rosebud pout. Pink cheeks. Her mouth was open. It was a dazzling little cave, dark red but glittering with pearls.

"I'm sorry, sweetheart," Diana said. "I..."

She'd never sworn in front of her daughter before. It was one of her personal, cardinal rules. Her own mother had never watched her language around Diana. She'd felt free to yell, "Asshole!" at other drivers while Diana rode beside her in their battered Ford, to say, "Fuck you," to phone solicitors before she slammed down the receiver, to call Diana's father a bastard to anyone who would listen, including his daughter.

Throughout Diana's youth she herself had cursed reflexively, thoughtlessly, and it had been one of the many things that had brought trouble upon her, or so it had seemed to her *after* the trouble, after she'd emerged from that staticky white space where she'd lived with her guilt and regret for a long time, pondering the trouble and what it was she'd done to bring it upon herself....

So, profanity was one of the first to go when she began to shed her bad habits. She'd not even sworn out loud to herself in... what?... A decade? Two?

She swerved around the minivan in front of her own and into the road. The driver, who was the mother of one of Emma's friends, honked angrily. In the silence inside herself Diana heard her own younger voice say, "*Go to hell,*" before she'd taken even a single second to think about it.

Heartbeat

She'd calmed back into herself before they even turned the corner to their neighborhood, which was a bright tunnel of green glass that afternoon. She was breathing evenly, and her heart had slowed to its normal *thrum-thrum, thrum-thrum.* She was herself again. Diana McFee. Wife. Mother. Content *woman-of-a-certain-age.*

The phrase amused her. She couldn't remember where she'd heard it, or why it had stuck in her mind. But now it was *her*... mother to a lovely little girl, wife of a respected professor, the woman she'd dreamed of becoming, whether or not she'd known it was her dream.

Perhaps, for a while, she'd had a different dream. Maybe she'd dreamed of being a model. She'd had the legs for it. And the high cheekbones. The teeth... she could have had them fixed. When she was young, she'd go into department stores and the sales people would say, "You should be a model," and she'd think, *Maybe someday.*

But time had passed with the sound of doors closing behind her—car doors, revolving doors, sliding glass doors, automatic doors—and she realized that the dream of being a model or a movie star was the kind of dream you might be able to take out of high school with you, driving a red convertible fast into your twenties. But after thirty, those dreams were dead.

That red convertible. You couldn't be a forty-year-old woman driving a red convertible. *This* dream—the silver mini-van, the daughter, the sparkling clapboard house—was the dream worth having.

When Diana McFee drove past Briar Hill High School, as always, she didn't look in the direction of the memorial to the victims, the bronzed angel with its wings spread and bearing the names of the twenty-four students and two teachers who had been killed....

Both girls are half asleep in the droning of Mr. McCleod's voice as he reads from the textbook to them.

Next to Mr. McCleod, the skeleton hangs in her absurdity, wearing a green bikini, holding a rose in her grim smile.

Twenty-two teenagers in the room, and no one makes a sound. Outside, it's pouring rain strangely icy for May, and it makes the classroom smell like the humid, private alcoves of the human body—crotches, underarms, the place where the shoulder meets the neck.

Never again in their lives will twenty-two strangers know one another as intimately as they do in this classroom. Passengers on a ship lost at sea for four years.

One of the girls rouses herself from her half-sleep and writes a note to the other. The note is about Nate Witt:

What's his best body part?

The note has to pass from Ryan Haslip to Melanie Burt to Nate himself, who passes it over to Michael Patrick without seeming, for even a second, to imagine that the note concerns him, concerns the great charge he sends off in two directions from the center of that classroom where he slumps and stares at the ceiling and thinks his brooding, magnetic, mysterious thoughts.

Lips, the other writes under her friend's question, and the note begins its journey back.

Mr. McCleod looks up from his textbook and sees Michael Patrick handing a folded piece of paper to Diana Allen.

He rises from his gunmetal desk and intercepts the note before Diana Allen can take it from Michael Patrick's hand.

Mr. McCleod's yellow fingers unfold it, trembling. He reads the note, tucks it into his shirt pocket, returns to his desk, to the open book on it, and begins to read from it again.

He says nothing about the note.

Mr. McCleod, however, has blushed.

IT WAS BREATHTAKING, THE NEIGHBORHOOD IN JUNE.

The shade trees that lined Maiden Lane were hundreds of years old. They leaned gracefully over the road like brides bent under the weight of their veils, and the sun pouring through them cast a strange green light that was only here and there broken by a blinding crack of brilliance. Those cracks left dark black slashes across Diana's vision until she blinked a few times or rubbed her eyes.

She needed sunglasses, she thought. In the Midwest it was never until summer that one thought to buy a new pair of sunglasses.

"Honey-bunny?" she said to Emma, who'd been riding beside her in silence, staring out the passenger's side window.

Diana patted her daughter's knee.

It was an oddly cold, sharp knee. Emma was so little, yet she was growing swiftly. It was as though her bones were growing too fast for her flesh to keep pace, as if they were close to being exposed beneath the soft, stretched skin. That skin was so familiar to Diana, it might as well have been her own. In a way, it was her own. Emma had come out of her body wearing that skin one afternoon eight years before.

But the bones... Diana didn't know her daughter's bones the way she knew her skin. When Emma was a baby, her bones had seemed soft and lost inside her skin. Impossible to imagine. Like the skeleton of a cloth doll, like scaffolding inside a cloud.

But now Emma was more like a toy poodle than a baby. A softness full of edges. *Muppet*... who was Muppet? Diana remembered, suddenly, someone's dog in her lap, quivering and full of bones.

Muppet.

Muppet was Maureen's dog. He had gray fur and smelled like corn chips. Maureen used to take him in her lap and press her face into the fur. The dog had brown tearstains in the corners of its eyes, and when it wasn't quivering in Maureen's lap, it was lying on the floor and licking its penis or growling at the crack under the front door when people passed in the hallway of the apartment building where Maureen lived with her mother.

Something ran into the road fast, and on four legs, and Diana swerved. A red blur—

Fucking squirrel.

Though she swerved, the squirrel ran straight under the minivan, and Diana instinctively closed her eyes. When she opened them, she saw the squirrel dash straight up a skinny sapling on the other side of the street. The tree shivered with the frantic weight of it, and the squirrel seemed to turn in the branches and watch Diana drive away. That squirrel's death. It would be back.

Diana exhaled, put her hand to the side of her face, and looked at Emma.

Fucking squirrel.

At least Diana hadn't said it out loud.

"Squirrel," Diana explained. She was shaking. Her heart was beating hard.

"Did we kill it?" Emma asked.

"No," Diana said. "It made it to the other side."

Emma nodded.

She hadn't seen it. Maybe she didn't even believe that there had been a squirrel. Emma was the kind of child who would weep if she saw a dead raccoon at the side of the road. She'd *never* been in a vehicle that had actually struck and killed an animal. Diana could only guess what her reaction would have been.

She drove a little slower.

Her palms were sweaty on the steering wheel, and the green light hurt her eyes.

Again she patted her daughter's cold knee.

Emma didn't look at her.

"Sweetie?" Diana said. "Look at me."

Emma turned obediently to look at her mother. Those blue eyes.

Whose were they?

Hers?

Her mother's?

Diana felt she was being appraised by them, dispassionately but with clarity. The swearing, the swerving, it must have made quite an impression on little Emma, who had never sat so still and quiet on the drive home after school.

Diana cleared her throat, still looking into her daughter's eyes, which were a paler blue than the sky, but made of the same substance as sky.

"Honey," Diana said, "I'm sorry if I was acting funny, and said bad words. I don't know what was the matter with me!"

She smiled at her daughter, and Emma smiled back. It was a small smile, but it indicated forgiveness. Diana felt a rush of something as fast and reflexive and helpless as that squirrel in the road. It had to do with love, of course, but love for her daughter didn't come in rushes. This had to do with the great, unexpected *mercy* of love. That tiny, unemotional but infinitely pardoning smile on her daughter's face...

She swallowed, and the feeling passed.

"Mommy," Emma said with her usual brightness. "Don't forget about the zoo. You're driving aren't you? Remember? The whole third grade is going to the zoo."

"Oh, my gosh," Diana said. "I almost did forget. When?"

"Not tomorrow," Emma said. "The next day. Friday. Our last day of school."

Emma leaned over and pulled a Xerox of a permission slip out of her Snow White backpack. Right under her name, *Emma McFee,* which Diana had written on her backpack in indelible black ink, Snow White had a little bluebird perched on her finger. It was an image that was burned into Diana's brain from her own girlhood. It had seemed to her, at Emma's age, the very image of purity, of girlhood... to be able to hold a bird that close to your face and to speak to it in such a hushed sweet voice that the bird would be enchanted, that the bird would lean closer to hear your soft song instead of flying away.

Even then it had been an old image. It had already endured much, but here it was on her daughter's backpack, born again.

At the bottom of the permission slip, which Diana had already signed—she recognized her own handwriting, loopy and girlish, which hadn't changed since she was in junior high—it said *I can drive* beside a box that was to be checked off by the willing parent, who was, in this case, Diana.

Always Diana checked off those boxes, even if it meant canceling a class at the community college where she taught. Her daughter (how well she knew it!) would only be a child for a short time, and Diana wanted to be involved in her life in every way and at every stage before that childhood was over. She remembered, vividly, her own eight-year-old self wearing a tinfoil crown, standing on a stage, scanning the crowd of parents for her mother's face, knowing her mother wouldn't be there because she couldn't afford to take time off from her job as an administrative assistant to come to her daughter's class play.

But still Diana stood there with that weightless crown on her head, hoping.

It was something, she'd long ago vowed, that would never happen to her own daughter.

"Well, now I remember, Emma-o," Diana said. "Of course I'll drive."

"Great!" Emma said. "I want Sarah Ann and Mary to ride with us."

Diana smiled and nodded. She said, "If that's okay with Sister Beatrice, it's okay with me."

Sarah Ann and Mary were Emma's best friends, and she'd been fiercely loyal to them, to the exclusion of all other girls, since kindergarten. The spring before, Emma's second-grade teacher had pulled Diana aside at a school open house to say she thought it would be nice to encourage Emma to make friends with some of the other girls, that maybe those three girls had become a bit too close for their own good.

The teacher had been a thick-ankled woman in her mid-twenties.

Mrs. Adams.

She wore smocks and jumpers, and for at least eight months Diana had assumed it was because the teacher was pregnant. But the teacher never grew larger, and she never gave birth. Her hair was so straight and white blond it seemed transparent, and she spoke in the voice of a child herself—a kind of silly singsong that seemed peculiar to the elementary-school teachers Diana had met at her daughter's Catholic girls' school, the ones who weren't nuns.

The nuns, in contrast to the other women, spoke to the children as if commanding a small, restless army. An army of cupids.

Diana had stood in the large shadow of that teacher at the school open house that night, with a cocktail napkin full of sugar-cookie crumbs in her hand, smiling politely. But she'd disregarded the teacher's advice.

It seemed to her—and to Paul, when she discussed it with him—that as long as they were polite, honest girls, it was none of their business who their daughter chose to befriend or how close those friendships became.

Too, it had been the spring that Timmy died, and both Paul

and Diana speculated that one of the reasons Emma clung so tightly to her two friends just then was because of the loss of Timmy. He'd been only a cat, but Emma had loved him, as she loved Sarah Ann and Mary, with a true and exclusive passion.

Diana could already tell that Emma, at only eight years old, was the kind of girl capable of passionate love, the kind of passionate love that might have caused an older girl, like a character in a tragedy or an old Scottish ballad, to throw herself from the cliffs onto the rocks, to allow herself to be tied to stakes, to rise from the dead to haunt the place where she'd lost the one she loved.

But Emma was only eight.

After Timmy had died, she simply refused to eat anything other than Cheerios and toast for a week, woke up screaming in terror for several nights, wept through the rooms of their house, looking under the couch and the chairs for Timmy long after Paul and Diana were sure their daughter understood that he was dead, and what *dead* meant.

Diana had brought Timmy's body in a cardboard box back from the veterinarian, and Paul had buried him in the backyard. Although they decided it would be too traumatic for Emma to actually watch her beloved cat being placed in a dark hole in the ground, they showed her where his grave was, and she and Diana had planted pale blue violets there. The violets had little human faces and seemed to crane their necks toward the world fearlessly, full of good humor, blown around gently on their thin green stems, fed by Timmy's moldering.

Still, whenever they mentioned the possibility of getting a kitten, Emma would say simply, "Timmy doesn't like other cats."

For two weeks, Mr. McCleod laughs easily in class.

He closes his book and speaks to the class from his heart about his love of biology, about the difficulties of finding a teaching position, about how he almost gave up and got a job in the auto-parts plant before he found this job, about the deep satisfaction he finds in coming to work at Briar Hill High every day.

The girls try not to look at one another.

It would only lead to laughter.

Laughter might hurt Mr. McCleod's feelings.

But they can feel one another thinking and full of laughter, a sea breeze across the biology classroom.

One day, a few weeks before the end of the school year, they come into the classroom before Mr. McCleod gets there. Ryan Haslip is at the blackboard. He writes *SLUT* on it with a piece of chalk the color of Mr. McCleod's teeth. He draws an arrow from the word to the skeleton, and then he takes his seat.

No one makes a sound when Mr. McCleod comes in.

It is a moment in which a small good could triumph over a small evil. The world is always poised, waiting before such moments. In this one, someone could jump up from his or her seat, take the eraser, and erase the word before he sees it.

But the silence is full of static....

A light rain begins to tick against the windows, although it's perfectly sunny outside, like an admission of guilt.

The word on the blackboard is the first thing Mr. McCleod sees, and he picks up the eraser himself and wipes it away.

He wipes furiously.

There's a pale yellow cloud of chalk in the air around him when he's finished.

When he turns to look at the class, his face is terrible, but he says nothing.

The next day, the bikini and the rose are gone from the skeleton, and Mr. McCleod gives the class an impossible, damning pop quiz on the three different types of the six hundred and forty muscles of the human body. One of them—the body's strongest—is the heart, and though he'd told them this fact over and over, not a single student gets it right.

Too young, too young.

REMEMBERING THAT—TIMMY TURNING TO VIOLETS IN the dirt—Diana turned the minivan onto Maiden Lane, and there was a moment in which a space parted between the tree branches overhead, and she caught a glimpse of the sky through the windshield.

It was absolutely clear and without a center.

The transparent vacuum of it startled her, and then the trees bent together again, blocking the empty blue, and she pulled into her own driveway and saw her husband sitting on the front porch in a white wicker rocking chair, waiting.

There were two of them—two rocking chairs. One was rocking emptily in the breeze beside the one in which her husband sat. They'd been part of the dream of the life she'd someday have. For years those very same rockers had sat on the front porch of a house down the block from the apartment building where Diana lived with her mother. Every winter they'd disappear, but every spring they would return, freshly painted. And even though Diana never actually saw anyone sitting in them, as she and her mother sped past them, the rockers spoke to her gracefully about the nature of *home.*

By coincidence she and Paul had just bought *their* home, many years later, when Diana drove by that same house on a Saturday morning and saw a sign out front that said ESTATE SALE.

She bought the rockers.

Now her husband was sitting in one of them. The intricate wickerwork rose above his shoulders and settled into gentle curves behind his back, exactly like a pair of wings. He was drinking from a can of Mountain Dew and waved hello with great exaggeration for Emma's benefit, an absurdly happy clown smile on his face.

Diana drove past the vision of her husband sitting in a white wicker rocker and into the garage, where she parked beside Paul's beat-up Schwinn. The minivan was their only vehicle because Paul rode that dust red Schwinn to his office and classes at the university, and the sight of him every morning rolling down the driveway into the road was one of Diana's favorites:

The gray-bearded philosophy professor in a tweed jacket and jeans, a pair of wire-rimmed glasses, pedaling furiously into the sun, the rain, even the snow.

Diana opened the driver's side door and stepped out of it into the garage, which smelled of oil-soaked rags. It was narrow as a coffin, and she could only just squeeze herself out of the minivan because the door wouldn't open all the way. Stepping down into the darkness, for just a moment she remembered being a child, easing her way into a lake, and how the silt and seaweed under her bare feet had given way suddenly to nothing and she'd found herself floating in shadows. Someone had been urging her forward... *Come on, Diana, don't be a chicken*... and then she was swimming.

Emma jumped quickly out of the minivan and hurried out of the garage, and Diana followed her, blinded by the late afternoon sun bouncing off the house and its bone-white clapboard.

"Hi, honey," she called into the glare in the direction of her husband.

"Hi, sweetheart," he called back from behind the wall of light.

Daisies

Rounding the corner toward her husband, Diana noticed that the daisies she'd planted years before off the sunny side of the porch were already flourishing wildly in the warm weather, smelling like a musty salad and spreading like... like what?

A cancer?

She stopped to look at them.

What would make her think, she wondered, suddenly of something like cancer, and find the fusty-earth smell of those daisies suffocating?

"How are my gals?" Paul asked, and Diana was startled away from the daisies and whatever ugly message they might have been trying to send. She could see that on the porch Emma was giving her father one of her mighty hugs. She was sitting on his lap. It was a picture of perfect father-daughter familiarity. *Family,* Diana thought as she stood and watched their embrace. Her daughter's small arms were flung around his neck. His eyes were closed. A crack of light broke through the green leafiness of their front yard, and it shone all over the two of them. The brightness of it caused her eyes to fill with water.

Family . . . famine . . . mine . . .

The words trailed across her eyes as if they were moving along one of those neon bars they used to have on buses, telling you what the next stop would be. STATE STREET . . . MAIN STREET . . . WESTLAND PLAZA . . . Until that moment, it had never occurred to Diana that the words bore any relationship to one another. Strange, she thought then, how associations came and went, making their odd revelations, as if thoughts were independent of their thinkers. Freud could have explained it, she supposed. Or Mr. McCleod, her high school biology teacher. Everyone else just let them come and go.

After school the girls walk to Burger King.

There, they'll lock themselves in the one-stall bathroom and change into the cutoffs they've crammed into the bottoms of their backpacks.

Winter lasted a long time, and now that the sun has finally risen once more over the slush and frozen grass of early spring, the heat of it seems closer to the earth than it's ever been. . . .

A burning, benevolent presence above them. At school even the teachers seem giddy. They start classes late because they're standing in the hallways talking to one another long after the bell has rung. In the hallway there's a cool, snaking breeze that winds from one end of the tunnel of it to the other, skimming over the gold-flecked linoleum and past the gray metal lockers.

Outside, the birds roll around in the puddles, and the squirrels dash down the green hill that slopes away from Briar Hill High into the street. They are trying to chase one another into the branches of the trees on the other side of the road. Usually they make it, but occasionally one of them is made into a small bloody rug under the wheels of someone's mother's station wagon or SUV.

Crossing the parking lot on their way to Burger King, they see Amanda Greenberg sitting on the trunk of her father's BMW, swinging her long legs, which are bare beneath the short black skirt she's wearing. She's a senior. She's just been elected Mayqueen, which is Briar Hill High's version of prom queen... the girl who'll wear a white gown and preside over the last dance of the year in the high school gym....

Four boys are standing around the Mayqueen in a semicircle. She throws her head backward with laughter, fast and hard, the way you'd swallow a big pill.

She is terrifyingly beautiful. An arrow of beauty. Her mother is black and her father is Jewish, and the union of those two has produced a face that is at once ancient and entirely new—long pitch-black hair, dusky skin, and eyes so blue and acute they're hard to look at.

She never notices the two younger girls walk by.

Next year one of those younger girls will be Mayqueen, but no one has even begun to dream of that yet.

"I HAVE GOOD NEWS," PAUL SAID, LOOKING AT DIANA over their daughter's bright head.

The sun numbered each one of Emma's golden hairs.

Diana stepped up onto the porch, and her shadow fell on her family.

"What?" Diana asked.

Paul looked excited. His eyes were wide. It was comic and adorable, that look of a happy child on the face of this professor. Her love for him, welling up, made her chest hurt. She put her hand flat against her ribs, and behind them she could feel her heart like a wingless bird in that cage.

"Tell me, sweetheart," she said.

Paul cleared his throat and tried to sound serious, though he was smiling widely. He said, "Your faithful servant here has been asked to give the Arthur M. Fuller lecture at the university in the fall."

"Oh, Paul," Diana said. She moved her hand from her chest to her mouth in a gesture of wonder and enthusiasm, but there was a chemical smell on her palm—something cleaner than soap—and she moved the hand away fast, wiping it on her black pants.

"Oh, Paul," she said again. "I'm so proud."

It was an incredible honor. The Arthur M. Fuller lecture was usually reserved for celebrities, dignitaries, or famous and elderly scholars from abroad. It was almost unthinkable that it would be given to one of the university's own. It was, certainly, the highest honor of Paul's career, which had been studded with prizes and awards.

"What are you going to talk about, Daddy?" Emma asked.

Emma knew that *lecture* meant talking. She'd already sat, fidgeting, through a few.

"Well, honey-bunny, I'm not sure yet, but you'll be the first expert I consult, okay?"

Emma jumped off Paul's lap to chase a black butterfly, which had fluttered out of the daisies and into the late-afternoon stillness sliding over the McFees' front lawn.

The Burger King smells like burning flesh and French fries, and the boys behind the counter smile at them when they step out of the bathroom in their cutoffs. . . .

There are paper Burger King crowns lined up near the cash registers, and one of the girls takes one, settles it precariously on her head.

"Mayqueen!" the other one says, and they both laugh.

One of the boys who works behind the counter at Burger King has only one arm. He smiles. The one empty sleeve of his uniform dangles like a ghost arm at his side.

Both of the girls flirt with him, not just out of pity. He has a bright, eager face and a gentle laugh. He flirts back with the girls from a distance, his olive-green eyes never meeting theirs. At first they think this reserve is due to his being at work, but when they walk away with their French fries and diet Cokes, they see him turn to his coworkers and pretend to be shot, grabbing his stomach with his one hand and collapsing onto the linoleum while the others laugh.

"He must have a girlfriend," one of the girls says.

Both girls are used to being flirted with, especially when they've initiated the flirting. They aren't conceited girls. They are simply both very beautiful and very young, and they have no idea that not every girl in the world is treated by men and boys with such intensity and attention.

They take their diet Cokes and small paper envelopes of French fries out to the Burger King parking lot, sit on the curb, stretch out their legs and let them shine in the sun.

Both girls will turn seventeen within the next few months, old enough now to get pregnant, to get jobs, to drive cars (neither girl has one yet, and one of the girls has never been allowed to take driver's ed)—they could even get married with their parents' permission—but neither will even be expected to get an after-school job. Their mothers feel too guilty about their girls' childhoods to let them work now....

All those years spent in day care or with baby-sitters while their divorced mothers worked and dated and took classes at the community college—their daughters are now being compensated for those years by being given all the money they need and vast stretches of unoccupied time.

They don't have much to do except wait for something to happen in that vastness.

They eat their French fries slowly. The salt and grease taste good, but they don't need to savor it. Neither girl needs to worry about her weight. The world is still full of French fries—fatty and golden and inexpensive. The *future* is rich with food... as much as they want of whatever they want, forever. They've seen their mothers measuring out portions of cottage cheese and skinless chicken breasts, but it's never crossed their minds that such a time in their own lives might come.

The lot of the Burger King begins to fill with cars. Those cars have to drive past their brilliant legs to park.

From a silver sports car, two ugly men emerge and walk together toward the restaurant entrance. Neither of the men is talking. They're wearing suits with loosened ties, and one of them has a thin mustache. They both look unself-consciously at the girls' legs as though the legs were attached to nothing, and both girls begin to laugh so hard at the absurdity of it that a young mother—she has a toddler dangling from one arm and a Teletubby diaper bag dangling from the other—gives them a dirty look.

All the young mothers glance angrily at the girls, whether they're laughing loudly or not. Also the middle-aged women with their prepubescent sons in football uniforms:

Those women glare over the clattering shoulders of their boys in the direction of the laughter.

The girls try to lower their voices, glancing nervously at those women, but within a few minutes they are screaming with laughter again.

Neither understands that the sight of them—long legged, sixteen, utterly free to scream with laughter in the parking lot of a fast-food restaurant in the middle of the afternoon—might fill some women with . . . what?

Longing? Resentment? Regret?

Neither girl has ever been an older woman, but every older woman has been a girl.

SHE'D MADE LINGUINE FOR DINNER, WITH HER OWN tomato sauce.

She'd bought a bushel of California Reds that morning from the fruit-and-vegetable stand operated every summer on the outskirts of Briar Hill by an elderly Mexican man and his elderly wife.

They'd been there every summer selling fruits and vegetables at the same junction between M-50 and the Blue Star Highway for twenty years, or longer—ever since Diana had been a child, buying with her mother identical bushels of tomatoes.

And the couple had always looked old, immortally old, to Diana.

They never spoke, only handed over whatever was requested of them and took the money for it coldly.

But Diana didn't mind. It was the fresh produce she went to that corner for... the apples, the tomatoes, the peaches. She'd been on one diet or another since Emma was born, and it was hard work, every day, watching what passed between her lips, to stay the same weight she'd been *before* Emma was born—a vigilance, a self-discipline she'd never imagined she'd have—and it wasn't until June, when the fresh fruits and vegetables came back, that Diana felt again what she'd once taken for granted: Eating and guiltless pleasure were relatives.

"Delicious!" Paul said.

And it was—the tangy freshness of the tomatoes, the sun and swelling still in them—but Paul always said that.

Diana was a good cook but not nearly as good as Paul made her out to be. When she'd meet his colleagues for the first time, they'd always say, "Oh, Diana, the incredible cook!"

At department parties his students would tell her that he often talked in class about what a great cook his wife was.

Diana watched her family eat the meal she'd made. Paul ate the linguine slowly, relishing, looking up now and then to smile, but Emma only twirled the linguine warily around and around the prongs of her fork. It was a phase, Diana and Paul had decided, this picking instead of eating, this playing with the food to avoid having to consume it, or at least to buy time until eating it. Paul and Diana thought, however, that it was best not to make much of it. Both of them had bad childhood memories of being forced to eat broccoli, or lima beans. Diana could still remember the deep soul-shudder she felt when she was forced to swallow a spoonful of casserole, globbed with cream of mushroom soup, her mother had held for what seemed like hours to her mouth—the cold sweat that broke out on her brow, and her mother, exasperated, saying, "Oh, *come on,* Diana."

"Don't you like your linguine?" Paul asked Emma.

She looked up at him and smiled weakly.

"Try it," Diana urged her, trying not to sound overly interested in whether or not she did. "The sauce is homemade."

Emma looked from one of her parents to the other, then at her fork massed with pasta. Tentatively, she put the fork to her mouth, kissed at it like a fish.

Then she looked up, seeming relieved, and let the linguine pass between her lips. She chewed, swallowed, then went for another bite of linguine, then another.

Emma ate a plateful of linguine.

"Well, I guess we've finally found something the picky eater likes!" Paul said, passing the plate back to Emma after putting another helping of linguine on it.

"This is good," Emma said, digging in again. She ate so fast that there was tomato sauce on her face and on her hands.

"Whoa, sweetie," Diana said, "slow down a bit." She reached across the table with a napkin and wiped some of the sauce off Emma's sweet, dimpled chin.

Footsteps

After dinner Emma went to her room to finish a drawing she'd started the evening before. Maybe, Diana thought, all children spent most of their hours with paints and crayons and sidewalk chalk—by what other means could a child express herself?—but Diana also dared to think that for Emma, as it had been for herself, the artistic impulse might be something more, something out of which a whole life could be created.

For Diana, drawing had been her grace. Her salvation. At the end of her sophomore year in high school, the year she'd nearly been kicked out of Briar Hill High, the art teacher, Ms. Jacobs, had pulled her aside in the hallway between classes one afternoon.

Ms. Jacobs was a thin, intense woman, with cascades of dark wavy hair. She wore middle-aged-hippie clothes—scratchy sweaters, Birkenstocks and purple kneesocks, long Indian-print skirts. Diana had liked her from the wary distance at which she regarded all her teachers. Too many times she'd grown fond of a teacher only to get kicked out of the class later, for tardiness or poor attendance. The teachers always liked Diana at first because she was smart and polite and because she carried herself with an adult poise. But then, as Diana began to skip class, miss assignments, fall asleep, they'd dismiss her as another one of *those.*

Ms. Jacobs had spoken to Diana in the hallway as if she were her friend. "Diana," she said, "I was a crappy high school student. Art saved me. You're so gifted, maybe it could save you, too, if you took it seriously."

A few weeks later Ms. Jacobs held up one of Diana's drawings in front of the class—a dark charcoal drawing of a woman's face, angled so that her hair fell over her features. She could have been any woman. It was an image Diana had held in her mind for many years. An image that came to her some mornings when she woke up, an image she saw clearly in all of its shades and outlines before she opened her eyes.

Ms. Jacobs had said, "This is one of the best student drawings I've ever seen."

She pointed out the detail, but also the way crucial elements had been left out—mystery, implication. The students hadn't—as Diana feared they would, when she saw it was her drawing being held up in front of the class—snickered or sighed. Even the most cynical of the students—the ones who took art because there weren't any papers or exams—were silent, attentive to the thing Diana had made. A new part of her life began that day.

When Emma had been upstairs with her drawing for a while, and Paul and Diana had finished their glasses of red wine, they stood up from the dining room table and started to clean up the dinner mess together.

Diana went into the kitchen, and Paul cleared the table, bringing the dishes to Diana, which she scraped off into the sink, then rinsed. She flipped the garbage disposal switch, and it did its violent underworld chewing and swallowing. Then Diana switched it off and stacked the cleared plates in the dishwasher.

The kitchen, like the dining room, was small. The cupboards were plain and pine, like the dining room table, and Diana had decorated the walls with small painted plates—flowers, thistles, herbs. It had always been her idea to do this when she had a kitchen of her own... to start a little collection of something to clutter it with. She had hung a checkered curtain on the window above the kitchen sink.

While she was bent over the dishwasher sorting the knives—which needed to be pointed down in the silverware basket for safety's sake—from the gentler forks and spoons, Paul came up behind her and slid his hand up the back of her sheer blouse. He leaned over and growled softly into her neck.

Startled, Diana flinched and dropped a knife on the floor at his feet.

"It's just me," Paul laughed. "Did you think someone else had slipped into the kitchen?"

Diana laughed, shook her head. She picked up the knife, which was golden with margarine.

That growling... it was the sound Paul used to make when they were first together, back when they used to make love on the floor of his office or in the creaky single bed in her dorm room when her roommate was gone. Over the years that growling had become a signal, Paul's way of letting her know he'd want to make love the minute they were alone.

Diana turned around, put her arms under her husband's, and offered her mouth to his. She inhaled the sweet grass-smell of his beard and mustache. They kissed long and hard until they heard their daughter's bedroom door creak open above them and the sound of her feet padding across the hardwood floors.

Every night they talk to each other on the telephone for hours....

When their mothers ask them what they could possibly have been talking about, they tell them the truth—that they don't know.

Their voices travel across the town of Briar Hill into each other's bedrooms. The phones they hold to their ears are cordless, weightless. They catch the girls' voices out of air.

But the voices are so clear, it's as if there is *nothing* in between them. Not lawns, not gardens, not the walls of their apartment complexes, not a grid of streets with names like Maiden Lane and University Street and Liberty Avenue—streets they walk along every day, streets down which their mothers drive them to school.

Their hometown is only a small dot on a map, but it's their world. No other hometown has ever existed. They are only sixteen, and the universe is a smeary mess of stars above the small town where they buy their CDs and French fries, develop their crushes, form their friendships—like this one—which are all of history to them. The pyramids. The Hebrews wandering in the desert. The atomic bomb dropped on Nagasaki. None of it has ever existed until this place, until them.... If you asked them to find Algiers on a map, they'd giggle, though they are no more or no less superficial than any other American girls.

Sixteen.

They've never heard of the Magna Carta, but they know the intimate secrets of the stars....

Not the stars in the sky...

Alanis Morissette, Leonardo DiCaprio, Madonna, Britney Spears.

"Nate's going to ask you out. He was looking at you today."

"No way!"

"Really... he was staring straight at you."

"He was probably just staring out the window."

"Well, he was staring out the window, too..."

"My mother just said I have to empty the dishwasher."

"Call me back."

"Okay. Give me fifteen."

"Bye."

"Bye."

IT WAS A BLESSING AND A CURSE, THE SOUNDS THAT HOUSE made.

Like all the houses in the neighborhood, their house was over a hundred and fifty years old. Generations of families had lived and died in it.

Despite its echoes and groans, it was a solid house, painted a respectable farmhouse white. It was right in the middle of the nicest neighborhood in Briar Hill, the neighborhood in which the most successful of those associated with the university chose to live, and had since 1816.

Diana had seen black-and-white photographs of those first

academics living in the neighborhood when it was new. They were thin, formal people, it seemed. The clothes they wore looked stiff. They drove carriages instead of Volvos. Diana tried, but always failed, to imagine such people in her garden, in her dining room, in her kitchen at a table, studying their thick books by candlelight at night.

They were so long gone by now that they couldn't even be imagined. Who they were, what they'd known, the things they'd wanted while they were alive, the way they must have felt, as certainly as all people felt, that they would never die.

But here were their houses, still held up by their original hand-hewn beams, inhabited—how briefly!—by strangers.

It was a perfect house... a dream house! And the fact that every footstep taken in any corner of it echoed through the rest of the house seemed a small price to pay for the perfection.

Maybe even a *part* of the perfection.

Paul and Diana, still in one another's arms, listened to their daughter's footsteps until they stopped at the upstairs bathroom.

"Paul," Diana said then, looking at his face, "I'm so proud of you... the lecture."

"I have to admit I'm pretty damn pleased with myself," Paul said, grinning and narrowing his eyes, which were the twinkling blue of a boy's, though he was fifty-five years old.

Diana listened again. She said, "Do you hear Emma?"

Paul cocked his head in the direction of the stairs.

"Maybe," he said. "She's in the bathroom. We can still fool around."

He pulled her to him again, one arm locked hard around her hips. He looked behind him as if to double-check that no one was watching. Then he pulled her blouse out of her jeans and slid his hand up her back, under her black bra to her breast, and squeezed it gently.

They heard the toilet flush upstairs—the sound of water rushing through their house, then away from it—and Paul pulled his hand out from under her bra.

"Look what you did," he said, adjusting the erection inside his khaki pants.

Diana laughed. Her heart was beating hard, like the heart of a teenage girl. They were both flushed.

"Enough of this for now," Diana said, handing Paul a wet sponge. "Go wipe down the table, you devil. We'll finish up this business later."

Paul winked as he left the kitchen, taking the sponge obediently with him.

Diana put the kettle on the stove to boil water for tea. It was a warm-weather tradition. After dinner she and Paul would sip cups of hot orange-spice tea on the front porch, rocking in the wicker rockers while Emma rode her bike up and down the block in the fading light, the streamers on her handlebars whipping as she zipped past.

It was part of the perfect life, the life Diana never for one second took for granted.

Perhaps when she was younger than she now remembered being, she'd imagined the perfect life to be that of a movie star, a lounge club singer. Or maybe she'd imagined a millionaire husband and a penthouse in Manhattan, a limousine taking her from one glamorous party to another. A closetful of sequins. Flashbulbs snapping in her face.

But even then she must have known that *that* wasn't it—

This was it.

Love. Family. Security.

Tonight they'd drink tea that tasted sweet and bitter at the same time, and in the morning she'd scramble eggs for Emma, drive her to school. A little later she'd go to the community college where she taught. It was the same community college her mother had attended when she was newly divorced and trying to imagine a life for herself, a life with improved computer skills and an associate's degree in something marketable, and bearable.

The irony of that never escaped Diana when she pulled up and parked her car in the faculty parking lot and carried her books and drawing pens into the college.

All those nights she'd been left alone or with her mother's boyfriend or a teenage baby-sitter while her mother went off to night classes at the mysterious college, which was going to change their lives . . . Diana was a teacher there now.

The computer skills and the associate's degree, of course, *hadn't* changed their lives. Diana's mother had stayed in the same low-paid clerical position in the philosophy department at the university until she retired.

But those nights . . .

The teenage girls who baby-sat would let her eat Pop-Tarts for dinner. They'd talk on the phone until Diana fell asleep in front of the television. *Buffy the Vampire Slayer* would turn the material world into a place full of magical evil. Diana dreaded that place while understanding too fully that she was already in it.

The baby-sitters would toss the blankets over her, and then she would be wide awake in the dark. When she'd hear her mother's keys jangling outside the apartment door, a hot fluid would spill inside her chest.

"Why do you always cry when I come *home*?" her mother would ask. "Other kids cry when their mothers *leave*."

Diana always knew, as she parked her minivan in the shadow of that college, that something had happened to her for which she needed to be eternally grateful. Something having to do with luck, with grace. She knew, too, that she'd done things to get this life, to have it . . . choices she'd made, words she'd uttered . . . images of them in her mind, faded like newspapers left on the front porch of people who'd left town without notifying the paperboy, left in the rain and the sun. Most of the time she couldn't even remember what these sins were, only that they'd been, and now they weren't, and now this life—this perfect life—was hers.

The kettle began a piercing scream, and Diana hurried to the stove and turned the gas off under the water, snuffing the crown of blue thorns and the scream at the same time. But then she heard above her another cry. This one was weaker, farther away. A cry followed by, "*Mama.*"

"Paul?" Diana called. "Emma?"

She hurried out of the kitchen. The sponge she'd handed Paul was on the dining room table, but he was gone.

She ran to the stairs and hurried up them. She stumbled, grabbed the railing, which was polished and slippery in her hand.

"Emma?" she called again.

Her daughter's bedroom door was open, but Emma wasn't in it.

The bathroom door was open, too, and Diana could see Paul's shadow in the hallway, a long shadow cast by the bright fluorescent light—a feature left over from the seventies, that unearthly tube above the sink. They kept meaning to change that fixture but never got around to doing it.

"Oh, honey," she heard her husband mutter. "Oh, sweetheart."

Diana could hear Emma whimper beyond him, a whimper that came from the painful brilliance....

She pushed past Paul into the bathroom, where she saw her daughter crumpled near the toilet, head resting against the porcelain tank, her white blouse and plaid skirt splattered with blood. Blood gushing from her mouth. Blood soaking her blond pigtails.

Diana lurched forward, unable to scream, dropped to her knees beside her daughter, thinking, *I have to stop the bleeding, I have to stop the bleeding*—

Then Emma reached over and touched Diana's hand with hers.

It was cold and clammy, her daughter's hand, and Diana gasped and pulled her own away.

That hand—it felt like clay.

There was a smell—cinnamon, nutmeg, curry, or?—

"She's sick," Paul said, looking at Diana pointedly. "Poor thing," he said. "All that linguine."

"Oh," Diana said. "Oh no," she said. She put her hand to her own neck. It seemed to her that the fluorescent tube above the sink surged, briefly, then became even brighter.

"Let's get you cleaned up, honey," Paul said to Emma, reaching past Diana to help his daughter to her feet.

Diana was still on her knees. Frozen in time, in place...

But what time? What place?

It seemed to her that her skin was slipping around on her like that light. Like a gown that was too large, shedding itself brilliantly down her arms. She put her hand to her forehead and tried to *pull herself together.*

It was just a headache. She recognized it then. It was the way her headaches arrived. It had been months since she'd had one, but now she remembered . . . the sense of being lifted by pain and brightness away from her body. If she took codeine now and lay down with an ice pack on her temple, by morning she'd be all right.

Emma reached out again and grabbed her mother's hand.

"I don't feel good, Mommy," Emma said weakly.

Diana opened her mouth but couldn't speak. Her own pain was shocking, an electrode at the base of her brain, at the tenderest place, the place where she felt love, had pleasant dreams, stored all the small happy moments of her childhood. A hot white branch inserted into that vulnerable place.

Her daughter's hand gripped her own too hard. It also hurt. Diana tried to pull her hand away, but her daughter just held on more tightly.

"Mommy," Emma said. "I'm sorry I threw up."

"It's okay, baby," Paul said to Emma.

He put the plug in the bathtub drain and started to run warm water into it.

"It's okay, Emma. Isn't it, Mommy?" Paul asked.

He looked at Diana with what she thought was disapproval.

All Diana could do was nod and move her lips as if she were saying yes.

Part Two

Thunder

Both Emma and Diana felt fine in the morning. There'd been a brief but violent thunderstorm in the middle of the night, and it had left the earth wet. Although Diana told Emma that she could stay home from school, Emma insisted on going. There were only two days of the third grade left that year, and it was Emma's "share day." She'd written a story about one of her dolls—Bethany Maria Anna Elizabeth—and was going to take the doll to school and read the story to her class.

On Sunday Diana had typed the story for Emma on Paul's computer, then printed it up on Monday in big bold letters that Emma could read easily. The story Emma told was that Bethany Maria Anna Elizabeth had been an orphan living in a convent until Emma found and adopted her. Emma loved Bethany Maria Anna Elizabeth, the story professed. The doll's favorite food was Froot Loops. The story ended, *She wants to be a mommy when she grows up.*

The only part of the story Diana had changed was a sentence that read, "Bethany Maria Anna Elizabeth HATES math tests and BORING science."

It had seemed a bit inflammatory to Diana. Already Diana felt that Sister Beatrice was a bit suspicious of Paul and herself—the academic and the artist—although Emma was certainly not the only non-Catholic at Our Lady of Fatima Elementary School, the only all-girls school in the area. As the Briar Hill public schools had grown larger and wilder over the years, with regular drug busts and a few isolated but stunning acts of violence, more and more parents were sending their children to the few private schools in town, and Our Lady of Fatima had had a boom in enrollment the likes of which it hadn't seen since the fifties. Emma was certainly not the only non-Catholic, but she might have been one of the few with no religious affiliation at all.

Paul had no interest in religion. He was interested in *thought. Where does the brain stop and the mind begin? If there is such a thing as evil, can there be such a thing as free will?*

And although Diana had interest in religion—a vague sense she'd always had, especially at dusk, that there was a presence she might have been able to communicate with if she knew the right words or could find the right place—she had no direction in which to point the interest. Her own mother had never even mentioned religion, and if she'd held any beliefs about what happened beyond this world or what happened after it, she'd kept them to herself. Church, the Bible, Jesus—from the distance at which Diana had caught the occasional glimpse of them—had seemed exotic and vaguely threatening. Secrets.

Rituals. Mysteries. She imagined fog, red velvet, the smell of the baking aisle at the grocery store—black pepper, brown sugar, oregano. Those scents were ones she'd associated with the strangeness of religious belief ever since she'd seen, on one of those Sundays, a little girl in a white lace dress and veil in that aisle at the grocery store, holding the hand of her mother, who was picking out spices.

The girl was no older than Diana herself. But Diana was wearing overalls and a checkered blouse. She'd been going through a farm-girl phase because of a Disney video her mother had bought for her and which she watched every night while her mother read magazines. The heroine of the movie wore overalls, milked cows, and chewed on long pieces of grass, and Diana wanted to be *her*...

Until she saw this other girl in the baking aisle.

Diana must have been staring, because the little girl looked at her from behind the veil and said, "I had my first communion today."

Diana had no idea what communion was but felt something slide open like a window inside her. A bit of the mystery slipped in along with the smell of cloves before her mother told her to hurry up and the window slammed shut.

She didn't think about religion much again until high school, when she became best friends with a born-again Christian. By then (and by then she was only sixteen) Diana had slipped far into the world, done many things for which she was sure she could not be forgiven by even the most merciful of divinities. She had only the vaguest concept of what constituted a sin, but Diana knew she ought to keep her head low, that if there were a god watching, the god didn't smile when he looked down on her.

Maureen never tried to convert Diana, but she used to talk about Jesus, how he loved everyone, forgave everyone, died for everyone. She talked about it in such a private, inward way—with total supernatural understanding—that Diana felt fearful and jealous at the same time. Maureen's eyes were very dark and long-lashed, and when she talked about Jesus, whom she'd actually *seen,* Diana could see why Maureen's mother had forbidden her to go to the church where she'd been reborn.

Now, as a grown woman, the confusion Diana felt when she thought about God was *made* of that fear, along with the fog and red velvet she used to imagine. She carried it inside her like a small candlelit church right behind her ribs—a place full of muttering and blood, a place she didn't feel comfortable going even though it belonged to her.

And sometimes Diana suspected that Sister Beatrice, in her strange black robes—only her pasty white hands and face exposed to this world of the flesh—saw the flaw, as well as a catalog of sins. That didn't frighten Diana, necessarily, or make her feel ashamed. It made her feel, instead, as though some private moment or place of her own had been glimpsed by a stranger from a disinterested distance.

If there were a word for what it made her feel, Diana guessed the word would have been *hopeless.* It was similar to the emotion she felt when, on the nightly news, she saw a corpse being taken out of a car wreck or out of a bombed building on a stretcher.

There was no use trying to hide yourself then.

If the world wanted to see your secrets, stare at your corpse, it could.

But it was also because Sister Beatrice had this effect on Diana that she changed the provocative, anti-math-and-science sentence in her daughter's story to read, "Bethany Maria Anna Elizabeth does not like math tests or science as much as she likes ice cream!"

Then Diana folded the typed story into fourths and tucked it into Emma's backpack.

They go to a boutique downtown and have extra holes pierced in their ears. . . .

Three small red-glass rubies in the left and three fake but dazzling little diamonds in the right.

They take turns looking at each other in the sunlight when they step out of the boutique into the brilliant sun bouncing off the chrome and glass of the clean cars parked up and down the street.

There are bright silver streaks of light on the sidewalk, sent out like arrows from those cars, and the girls step into that shower of arrows wearing sandals, shorts, and tank tops. They hold each other's hair away from the new jewels, which shock and spark like miniature and glittering thoughts around their heads.

"Great," one of their mothers will say wearily when she sees them. "Just what you girls needed. A few more holes in your heads."

It's the first day of summer vacation.

IT WAS A DARK MORNING. THE THUNDERSTORM OF THE night had left the sky cloudy and the streets slippery with green leaves. Emma sat quietly, still half asleep, next to Diana in the minivan; Bethany Maria Anna Elizabeth sat on her lap. The doll had been a gift from Paul's mother—an expensive blond baby girl with bright blue eyes that shut when she was put down on her back for a nap or when she slipped from Emma's bed onto the floor while Emma slept. That doll wore a lacy white dress and had a fixed rosebud smile—or was it, Diana wondered, a bit of a smirk?

She pulled up in front of the school, into the semicircular drive. Little girls were being let out of cars, skipping up the concrete steps to wait at the orange double doors for the bell to ring, to be let into the school.

Diana felt homely in the gray sweat suit she'd pulled on that morning. She wore it often in the mornings but never without feeling like a fixed target in it. Fervently Diana believed that women didn't need to get dumpy when they got older, but here she was in a baggy sweat suit, without makeup. It was only to drive her daughter to school, she always thought, but by the time she was actually a few miles from her home, wearing this middle-aged mother's uniform, Diana felt conspicuous, ashamed.

But it didn't matter to Emma.

"I love you, Mommy," she said.

"I love you, too. Have a good day, Emma-o," Diana said, leaning over to hug and kiss her daughter good-bye.

Emma's breath smelled of chocolate milk. Her hair smelled of dreams and damp dirt. As she always did, nuzzling her daughter before bedtime or kissing her good-bye before parting, Diana felt a moment of physical longing like terror, like the moment she sometimes had just before sleep, not wanting to slip out of the sensual world no matter how sweet the dream that was waiting beyond it might be.

"What about Bethany Maria Anna Elizabeth?" Emma asked.

"Good-bye, Bethany Maria Anna Elizabeth," Diana said animatedly to the blank face of her daughter's doll.

"But she wants a kiss," Emma said, holding the doll up.

Diana leaned over and kissed the doll, whose cheek was cold.

Emma jumped out of the minivan and, with her Snow White backpack on, her pink jacket, her doll held like a real baby carefully over her shoulder, supported in the crook of her arm, Emma ascended the concrete stairs. Above her, at the orange double doors, the other little girls waited, pacing, looking pale in their plaid skirts and knee socks in the wavering dampness that had begun to warm and rise steamily up from the cement.

For a second Diana felt the urge to hurry after her, pull her back, keep her apart from that group, which looked somber to her from this distance—too serious, like sick girls. Too, they seemed to be watching Emma climb the stairs too closely, too anxiously, and Diana felt a terrible pang of possessiveness (*mine*) just before she heard the mechanical wildness of the school bell ringing and saw her daughter start to run. The orange double doors opened, and the little girls began to disappear into the shining darkness of the place where they spent their days.

Diana glanced one more time toward those doors before she pulled out of the semicircular drive, thinking she saw Sister Beatrice—in her black habit, smiling—take Emma by the hot-pink arm of her summer jacket and pull her through the open doors.

June.

It's still just June.

But time begins to slow down and the summer afternoons

become palpable, made of warm laundry and canned air freshener.

Their mothers go off to their jobs in the morning, and the girls never hear them leave. They sleep until noon, then rise and watch talk shows while eating bowls of cereal. The milk in their spoons is sweet even after the Froot Loops or Cheerios or cornflakes have been eaten.

One of them always calls the other by the middle of the raunchiest of the talk shows.

"Are you watching?"

"Can you believe it?"

They agree on a place to meet. Downtown in a coffee shop or a bookstore or the boutique where their ears were pierced.

They would rather go to the mall, but a bus would have to be taken to get there.

Downtown will have to do.

They can walk there from their mothers' apartments. In summer most of the students are gone, and what they've left is a humid breeze blowing the dry dirt and trash around by the curb, along with the street people playing their busted guitars, and the empty emerald beer bottles in the bushes.

Also in summer the restaurants and stores along East Main Street and University Avenue prop their doors open. The smell of incense mingles with the smell of *moo shu* pork. There are always a few young men—graduate students? Young professors?—sitting at outdoor tables eating egg rolls and reading library books.

The girls watch these men, speculate about them, but in the end those men are always joined by young women wearing wire-rimmed glasses and slim black jeans.

Still, now and then, one of them will look up from his library book and say hi in a way that might be an invitation for the girls to join him.

The girls say hi back in a way that lets him know they won't, and he returns to his book, angry or embarrassed.

IT WAS A QUIET MORNING. . . .

Only the squirrels and the mailman were out.

The squirrels were arguing among themselves—*Get over here, No, you get over here*—from opposite sides of the road, and Diana felt jumpy, watching them from behind the wheel of her minivan.

The apple and pear trees were in bloom. They looked ecstatic. Shot through with pleasure, from their green blood to their exploded blossoms. They looked like virgins about to be sacrificed, happily, martyrs—pagan, or prom queens, or brides of Christ—and they trembled in the cool and anticipatory breeze.

The mailman, crossing the street at the corner, took his cap off by the bill for a moment and wiped his forehead with his hand. Already it was warming up. His blue bag was stuffed with packages and letters. Something in there, Diana knew, had her name on it.

He'd been the mailman in this neighborhood ever since Paul and Diana had moved in. His name was Randall, a fact she knew only because Emma had asked him one Saturday morning and had promptly reported the information to Diana.

Diana thought Randall turned and looked at her as she drove by, still with his hat in his hand, but when Diana waved, he only looked blankly back at her.

He was a handsome man—middle-aged but very fit, deeply

tanned, with a full head of curly dark hair. And although he was still blocks from Paul and Diana's house, she knew he'd be on their front stoop soon. He moved through the neighborhood with otherworldly swiftness.

Turning the corner Diana saw that the house was for sale in which Mrs. Mueler had lived, and died, recently, of pancreatic cancer. It was a bungalow—an unusually modest home in that neighborhood—and it was painted light green. It had a large picture window that faced the street. A few times, walking around the block with Emma, or in search of Emma after she learned to ride a bike, Diana had seen Mrs. Mueler standing at that large window, looking out at the street—perhaps this was before the cancer, or while the cancer was still a secret kept deep in the pancreas of Mrs. Mueler—and Diana had waved brightly.

Mrs. Mueler waved back without smiling.

Once, Diana saw her in her front yard, kneeling. Diana said hello, and Mrs. Mueler turned around, startled, and said, "Good afternoon," although it was early dusk.

Diana was sure that Mrs. Mueler didn't recognize her or remember that she'd tried, in what seemed like another lifetime, to have Diana kicked out of Briar Hill High for carrying a Baggie of marijuana to school in her purse...

Still, Diana felt as though Mrs. Mueler, on her knees with a ball of roots and dirt, poised over a dark hole growing darker as the sun set, had looked at her suspiciously. And even though Diana held no grudge—why should she, knowing that she'd been more than deserving of the punishment Mrs. Mueler wanted to mete out?—she'd felt relieved of something, some small burden from the past that weighed no more than crushed leaves in a plastic Baggie but which had been weighing her down nonetheless for more than two decades, when she read in the paper that Mrs. Mueler had died "at home, after a long battle with pancreatic cancer."

FOR SALE, the sign in her front yard said now. The curtains in the picture window had been opened for the first time in years, and Diana saw someone move beyond them—a realtor? a relative?—as she drove by. A quick glimpse of a thin face.

When she pulled onto her own block, she was surprised to see Randall the mailman standing on the front steps. He was stuffing a large manila envelope into their box.

How could it be? Hadn't she just seen him five or six blocks over?

"Hi!" Diana called, rolling down her window as she pulled in the drive.

"Hello, ma'am," Randall said, but he didn't look at her. In the past he'd been friendly—not overly so, but friendlier than this. He'd never called her "ma'am." He knew, of course, her name.

"Didn't I just see you a few blocks over?" Diana asked.

Randall the mailman must not have heard her. He crossed the lawn between their house and the neighbor's without looking back, and Diana felt embarrassed, her mouth left hanging open for a moment until she consciously shut it and swallowed, watching him walk away, slipping between the shrubs quickly.

But not quickly enough to have walked five blocks in under sixty seconds.

A mistake.

Another mailman.

Or maybe she had never seen any mailman at all, only thought she'd seen one. Maybe she'd seen a *memory* of having seen Randall on some other summer morning—the morning before, or the *year* before. Randall had always been their mailman.

How many times had she seen him walking through the neighborhood, carrying a bag full of envelopes and catalogs? Maybe it was a simple synapse misfiring... a moment of confusion between one hemisphere and the other. It must have happened all the time. How often did people burn down their houses because they'd left something boiling on the stove, something they clearly remembered removing from the stove?

Diana rolled up the minivan window and pulled all the way into the driveway and parked in the garage, the door of which she always left open when she went out on a quick errand. It was probably not the best idea, since there was a key to the house hanging on a hook in there, right above the trash cans, where any thief would probably look first for a key to a house. And there was also a short flight of rickety plywood stairs that stretched straight from the garage to a room above it, the room which was her studio. The door to the studio didn't even *have* a lock.

But it was a neighborhood with so little crime that it was impossible to stay vigilant and not feel neurotic. The safety of the neighborhood encouraged complacence, and probably made them more vulnerable because of it. Yet Diana couldn't understand how a person could prepare for something that couldn't be imagined, something that had never been experienced, and could not have been expected...

Like a stroke, or a bomb, or a flash flood, or death.

Maybe some people could think that far ahead—like the emperor who'd had a whole army of terracotta soldiers and horses made to accompany him to the grave.

Maybe Mrs. Mueler had. Maybe she'd cleaned out her closets when she was diagnosed with cancer, so her relatives wouldn't have to. Some people, Diana knew, wrote the services for their own funerals, picked out their own cemetery plots.

And *those* people would have shut and locked their doors even in the safest of neighborhoods, even in a neighborhood in which there hadn't been even an act of vandalism in half a century.

Those people could have imagined it and prepared for it. But Diana couldn't.

Before she went in the house, she walked around to the front, to retrieve the manila envelope she'd seen Randall stuff into the box.

The sun had already made its way to the daisies, which looked crushed from the hard rain of the night before, but stirring, lifting themselves out of the damp dirt.

The front yard was littered with apple blossom petals, as if there'd been a wedding there in the rain, or a fight between two flower girls. On the lawn those petals looked like cool candle flames, or polished fingernails.

"Hi, Mrs. McFee!" a boy yelled as he rode his bike past their house, but by the time Diana turned to see who it was, the boy had blurred halfway down the block.

Who had it been, and why wasn't he in school?

She lifted the manila envelope out of the mailbox.

DIANA was written in large block letters with black Magic Marker on the front of it, and her address, in smaller letters, underneath:

1740 Maiden Lane

The handwriting seemed vaguely familiar. It reminded her of her own. She walked back around the side of the house, tearing open the gummed flap as she walked.

She glanced at the daisies as she passed. Not even nine o'clock in the morning and they were already stretching, lifting their big eyes to the sky. . . .

Inside the envelope, in the yellow shadows, there was nothing.

Diana held the empty envelope in her hand a long time.

The daisies, from the corner of her eye . . . she could almost see them writhing, trying—

She looked more deeply into the envelope, but still there was nothing. She looked at the front of it again. Her name, but no return address. Then she shook her head, crumpled the envelope up and took it into the garage, removed the lid from the trash can, which was empty but smelled of decay, and threw the envelope in. The trash can made no sound as the envelope dropped into the bright aluminum, but it shuddered when Diana put the top back on. She stepped back into the light, and then she thought about it again.

Envelopes contained letters. Envelopes did not arrive in mailboxes empty.

She went back and retrieved the envelope, turning her face away from the sweet stink of years of garbage gone but still lingering in the brilliant container, and pressed out the wrinkles as best she could, then looked inside it again.

This time she noticed a small scrap of paper at the very bottom of the envelope. A tiny piece of notebook paper folded into fourths. She took it out, pressed it flat, and walked with it out of the garage, where she could see it more clearly in the light.

In black ink, in big block letters: SLUT.

Something ran through her like a knife blade, but made of cool air, and she inhaled, turned the paper over, looked at it again.

That word. A word she hadn't heard or used in years but which used to mean something to her . . . about her.

She put her hand to her forehead, and it felt hot.

High school.

It hadn't been since *high school* that she would have cared whether or not she'd been called a slut. In high school that word was the worst thing a girl could be called, and that word was everywhere. It was in the water that came out of the drinking fountain, in the whisper of the paper-towel dispenser in the girl's bathroom—and the word had to do with *her,* with her body and its curves, with her dreams and desires . . . something having to do with the very essence of her, the sexual essence of who she was and was becoming—a physical creature, all five senses poised, bared, laid open, and condemned.

And then, simply, she went to college, where everyone had sex, everyone had sexuality—bisexuality, homosexuality. They gave you condoms with the key to your dorm room.

Slut.

Miraculously, suddenly, the word had evaporated from the world. The word meant *nothing.* And then she'd gotten married.

And now . . . now it was almost a compliment, Diana realized, half smiling.

To be a forty-year-old woman in a gray sweat suit standing out behind her clapboard house having just dropped her daughter off at school, breakfast dishes waiting to be washed, the hood of her minivan still warm in the garage. . . .

To be a soccer mom someone might have taken the time to think of as a *slut.*

She didn't laugh out loud, but she smiled.

There was no sting in it, no life, and the realization came as a strange relief, a strange relief out of nowhere, like finding out you didn't have a disease you'd never suspected you'd had.

But who would have sent her such a note?

She looked at the handwriting again, but the more she looked, the less familiar it became. Finally she crumpled it all back up and again tossed it in the trash can in the garage, closing the lid tightly, walking away from it, still smiling.

It was certainly not worth worrying about.

Some crazy student of Paul's. Some student of her own from the community college, someone she'd failed for poor attendance, or someone who remembered her from high school—some old boyfriend she'd dumped.

She was forty years old. She'd lived in Briar Hill her whole life. The number of people she'd hurt or rejected, the number of times she'd said something cruel (though never intentionally—could she ever remember a time she'd *intentionally* hurt another person?) was unfathomable by now. It made her dizzy and sick to think of it, like looking into an abyss full of stink and flies. It wasn't the first time something like this had happened. Some inexplicable message intended to—what? Unnerve her? Disarm her?

She wouldn't let it.

Life was short.

Her life was perfect.

And it was *hers.*

Peonies and Lilac

Always with Emma off at school, the house seemed empty to Diana—though not unpleasantly so.

All the life that had taken place in it only an hour before—the toast, the coffee, the scrambled eggs, the pajamas tossed on the bedroom floor—all that life had accumulated a silence that seemed made of whatever dusty particles thought and memory sent out of the mind in the process of passing.

Nothing had happened there in the brief time between Diana's leaving with Emma and returning without her, and nothing would change now until Diana chose to change it.

The house was a still life....

A still life you could walk into and observe with all of your senses, the stationary images of your things, the silence and the material that made up your life.

Paul's spoon lying where he had left it beside his bowl of Grape-Nuts.

Emma's Pooh cup half full of Sunny Delight.

Diana stopped at that image and took a sip from the cup. The strange breakfast beverage in it—what was it made of, the juice of some hallucinated fruit?—tasted oddly cold, and the frozen sweetness of it opened a bright eye of pain at Diana's temple, and the pain of it placed her securely back into her body. She poured what was left of the juice into the sink and put the cup upside down in the empty dishwasher, then opened the back door and looked out into the yard.

A damp violet fog poured in through the screen door, filtered into a million little microscopic squares. But there was heat in the breeze. The sun was rising higher in the sky, and it was burning away the cool storm of the night before.

Diana stood very still, trying to remember something... Who?...What?

There was something (someone?) standing just outside of the reach of her thoughts, someone she needed to recall, who had been brought in on the warmed breeze but then been turned to molecules passing through the back door's screen. It was something that bothered her, some detail that was out of place in her dream-perfect life, something that, if she could reach it with her recollection, she might be able to return to its right place.

Miss Zena?

Miss Zena.

It must have been the peonies in their crisp tutus, just bloomed, that had reminded her—the ribbons and lace, the girly purity of it. Then, a little black cloud passing over the prettiness of her backyard. Diana never thought of ballet, of her pink satin toe shoes, without feeling shame.

For years she'd taken ballet lessons at Miss Zena's School of Dance, a studio owned by a French woman in a strip mall outside of town, and she'd loved it... loved the French woman, who was all grace and bones, loved ballet... but then she'd quit taking the lessons after ninth grade, after she'd gotten caught smoking marijuana with six or seven other ballerinas in the dressing room just before they were to go onstage for their end-of-the-year recital.

They were wearing black leotards, flesh-colored tights, hot-pink tutus that circled their hips and waists with stiffness. The auditorium was in one of the oldest buildings in Briar Hill. Heavy velvet curtains. Radiators knocking, leaking boiling water onto the dressing room's cracked ceramic tiles.

It was spring. The heat was unnecessary, especially with all those girls perspiring in their leotards, and it steamed up the dressing room mirrors.

They'd gathered in a circle and passed the joint around, the smell of cotton balls and the sickly sweetness of those burning leaves.

It hadn't been Diana's joint, and it hadn't been her idea, but there she was in the circle when Miss Zena, who must have been standing in the doorway for a while by the time she was noticed, said, crying a little, "It ees time for you to dance, you leetle beetches, you beetches who half broken my heart."

There was no time to talk then. Whoever had the joint tossed it away somewhere, and Miss Zena hurried them out to the back of the stage, which was dark and hung with ropes and discarded ballet shoes, sequins and tinsel scattered on folding chairs, and the heavy dust-smell of velvet.

The accompanist started to bang out their cue, then stopped, and the girls drifted into the stage lights. There were chalk circles drawn on the floor, and each girl moved into her own circle, the *swish-swish* of tutus in the silence.

All Diana remembered was the sensation of floating, a starburst in her eyes, and then it seemed as though there were little bits of glitter attaching themselves to her eyelids and arms. She had never smiled before with such unselfconscious joy. When she looked out at the audience of parents and siblings, she saw electric beach grass blowing in a breeze.

Wild applause when they were done.

Her heart was beating hard.

"That was beautiful," her mother said when she came to the dressing room to get her. "You girls are so talented," she said, speaking to them all.

They didn't look at one another.

Miss Zena never told any parents what had happened, as far as Diana knew, but none of the girls who'd gotten caught in the dressing room signed up for ballet lessons the next year. When her mother asked her why she was giving up ballet, Diana had simply said, "It's for little girls."

And even all these years later it still filled her with remorse and a terrible stab of loss to think about it. All those years of ballet lessons—Miss Zena scolding her about her derriere, her pliés and relevés, maneuvering her thin feet into satin shoes with cardboard toes, the tautness of ribbons around her ankles.

All that sweetness and grace had turned into one false and brilliant performance in her mind, a few fleeting and hallucinatory minutes of fraudulent bliss.

She narrowed her eyes, looking through that screen, then rubbed her eyes and Miss Zena was gone.

The backyard was scattered with Emma's toys—a Frisbee, a red wagon, a plastic pony on wheels, which had been bought at a garage sale when Emma was three and which she'd ridden wildly around the house for years, scuffing up the hardwood floors.

Then it was abandoned in the front hallway, near the coat closet, where it grazed absently for a long time . . . a stiff, blank-eyed thing they had to step around on their way to other places, a toy in a kind of limbo between rummage sales.

When Diana and Paul had suggested that they give the pony to the Salvation Army with some old bicycles, Emma had squinted at her parents as if they were people she barely recognized, people she wasn't sure she wanted to know better.

The pony was kept, although it was eventually sent out to the backyard, where it spent its days staring expressionlessly into the side of the garage. If it ever thought of them, of the lives they led inside the house without it, it could not have been with fondness. It had a few wet leaves stuck to its saddle and in its mane that morning.

Already the lilacs that grew in wondrous profusion near the back of the garage had gone brown. They'd bloomed fiercely throughout May, sending out a perfume that made Diana think of a funeral parlor or a prom dance.

One afternoon in the first week of July, they run into Nate Witt outside Big Mama's CDs & Tapes.

There are small yellow leaflets at his feet. He's looking at the back of the CD he's apparently just bought.

"Hi, Nate," one of them says.

Nate Witt looks up and says hi to the air, but he doesn't seem to see the girls.

They start to laugh, hurry past him, pushing each other and covering their mouths with their hands.

One of the girls is wearing an ankle bracelet, which makes the sound of jewel-box music as she runs.

They don't stop laughing until they're back at the apartment where one of the girls lives with her mother. There they turn the radio up loud. WRIP is playing a song by Nirvana.

They try looking up Nate Witt's telephone number in the Briar Hill phone book—paging through the thin, pulp-soft pages of tiny names—but there are eleven Witts listed there, and who knows what Nate Witt's father's first name might be, or even if Nate Witt has a father? The phone book makes a dusty sound when it's tossed back into its place on the coffee table next to the phone.

The girls lie around in the bedroom, which is full of stuffed animals and dolls—expensive ones, the ones that last past childhood because they were never dragged to day care or to the park or left at Daddy's house by accident on an overnighter.

At Daddy's house that doll might have been ruined by Daddy's other kid: a little boy who looks exactly like his mother and doesn't seem at all like a brother. He's shy, especially around strangers, but he'd have played hard with that doll's arms and legs, snapped her neck trying to bend her head backward so she could look up at the stars....

The dolls—one of them a perfect baby girl with blue glass eyes—and stuffed animals regard the girls stiffly, but without judgment, accumulating dust on the shelves. They never consider the future, which for them can't last much longer. What mother would keep such things around a small apartment after her grown daughter has moved out?

Outside there's the sound of traffic swooping by on the busy street.

Only half the day is over.

Not even half the summer.

It's a hot and odorless afternoon.

The blossoms of May and June have dried up or fallen out of the trees, but girlhood goes on and on.

"Why the hell didn't we stop and say something, ask him what CD he bought or something?"

"Because we're idiots?"

"Well, why are we idiots?"

One of the girls is lying on her back on the bed, balancing a lacy white pillow on her bare foot.

The other sits cross-legged on the floor.

"Because he's Nate Witt," she says.

THE SMELL OF FLOWERS. IT WAS THE VERY ESSENCE OF the month of June—the suffocating sweetness of flowers, the loose pastel scarves of scent slipping through the air, riding over the dampness and rot of spring.

By June she'd grown used to the smell of flowering. Though the flowers continued to bloom, they ceased to surprise. But in May, the lilacs had come on like a light in a cave. The scent of them brought back the scent of every flower she'd ever smelled. A little shock. A pin stabbing her just above the heart, a spray of baby's breath and pink roses pinned to her white prom dress. And she could remember, too, standing at the edge of her grandmother's white coffin, looking in, the smell of violets rising from the powdered hands.

Only a month ago the lilacs in the backyard had bloomed, then dwindled, and now they were brown corsages stuck into the shrubs near the back of the garage. New flowers—the peonies, rustling through the backyard in their tutus and toe shoes, and a wild vine of roses trained to climb the white fence that separated their yard from the neighbors'—had taken their place, accompanied by small and golden clouds of honeybees circling them, humming.

Humming

Diana McFee was no gardener, but she loved her little garden.

Every year she'd buy a few things at the nursery and plant them, and now they'd lived in the house long enough that those few things had accumulated and spread, taking on the appearance of a *real* garden, the kind she used to gaze down on from the sliding glass patio doors of her mother's third-floor apartment.

From that patio Diana could see the backyards of the houses all over the neighborhood, and the little tended Edens behind them. That apartment was only a few blocks from this very house. Perhaps one of the gardens she'd looked down on had been this very one.

Someday, she'd think...

And now she had her very own garden.

She didn't even mind the weeds. Occasionally she'd go out there with a scythe, which had never been sharpened, and whack something down that had begun to choke out the holly-hocks, but that was the extent of her war against weeds. Paul only mowed the lawn, or paid one of the neighbor boys to do it, about half a dozen times a year. It wasn't neglect, Diana wanted to believe. It was a form of respect. She didn't want to prune and fertilize and mow and weed her piece of the world until it no longer bore any resemblance *to* the world. She'd seen plenty of that kind of garden, and the women who tended them.

From where Diana stood at her back door that morning, she could see into the backyard of the Ellsworths, the neigh-bors who were separated from them by the white wooden fence on which the roses made their slow ascent.

The Ellsworths had neither lawn nor flowers, but had in-stead a swimming pool surrounded by cement. The other-worldly aqua blue made a strange backdrop to the bloodred of the roses, though the two colors didn't exactly clash.

The Ellsworths were the only people in the neighborhood with a pool. It had been just the weekend before that they'd taken the winter cover off of it and filled it with water, but Diana thought she could make out someone swimming in it already.

So early in the season, who could it be?

She knew that Sandy Ellsworth worked at the hospital, in the business office she thought, and Diana had always assumed that it was a nine-to-five thing. Sandy Ellsworth was about Diana's age, but the husband looked older. Diana had never ac-tually spoken with him, but she'd never seen him outside on a weekday, and he looked a bit too young to have retired. The couple had no children, at least none Diana had ever seen. Just a poodle with a human name—Ann; or was it Helen?—which escaped a few times every year. The Ellsworths would walk around and around the block calling her name frantically.

Day off, Diana guessed. Sick day. Personal day. One of the first really warm days of the year. Why *not* stay home and use the pool, which, in their climate, was only really usable for about ten weeks out of the year?

Diana admired them for it. They'd seemed too stern for such a dalliance. Their pool had always appeared mainly to serve the purpose of providing something around which the two of them could sit and have a drink together between six and seven o'clock on summer evenings. It had been an annoyance to Diana, the pool. She felt she had to be extra vigilant watching Emma lest she should wander into the Ellsworths' yard and fall into that pool. Diana knew it took only seconds for such a thing to happen. The phone rings, the kettle starts to whistle, you turn your back, and your child slips over that shimmering edge forever.

Only after Emma learned to swim did Diana begin to relax about that pool, where today someone was swimming, and it seemed like a good idea....

The sun shone brightly on the surface, and it glinted beyond the foliage and those roses that separated the yards—glinted like a blade, then dispersed, as if brilliant knitting were unraveling there. Then a dark mass surfaced in the aqua blue, rose up out of the supernatural blueness, and shook its head before diving under again.

Diana watched the figure dive and surface a few more times, and she wondered which of the Ellsworths it was. She was about to turn away when she heard laughter—a girl's—followed by a playful shriek, and then Diana saw the source of the laughter emerge from the Ellsworths' sliding glass patio doors.

She was naked.

A young woman?

A girl?

She had long blond hair, and Diana could see her pale breasts and a triangle of blond hair between her legs.

Whoever was swimming in the pool shouted to her, "Get the fuck in here," in the voice of a man. A young man. He must have reached out and grabbed the girl's ankle when she stepped up to the side of the pool, because Diana saw arms flailing as the girl lost her balance and splashed into the screaming brightness.

Diana took a step backward, back into her kitchen, the shadows of her home.

Who could they be?

Diana couldn't imagine the Ellsworths having relatives who would swim naked in their swimming pool in broad daylight, but neither could she imagine a couple of teenagers having the audacity to sneak into a stranger's pool—naked, shouting.

She watched for a few more minutes, but the giggling and splashing had gone silent. Diana could still see them, though—two figures made of flesh gliding smoothly down the center of the pool, holding on to one another.

They were kissing, Diana realized, and then she realized they were also—must have been—having sex. The way the girl was rising and falling against the body of the boy.

It surprised her, the shock and anger she felt.

She turned quickly from the kitchen door and closed it behind her, then headed toward the stairs, grabbing things as she went—pencils and napkins and coloring books—to return them to the places they belonged.

Her heart was beating hard. She could hear it in her ears. For a split second, passing by the telephone, she considered calling the police.

But what if the teenagers in the pool were friends or relatives of the Ellsworths—his grown son from a previous marriage and a girlfriend, perhaps?

Then it would seem that it was simply the nudity, the sex, that had prompted a call to the police. Diana would seem to be not only a prude and a busybody but a voyeur, for how would she have noticed the nudity and the sex if she hadn't been watching the neighbors' backyard carefully, from behind her own screen door? Had she been outside where they could see her watching, they would most likely have refrained from engaging in such behavior.

Such behavior, she imagined herself saying to a police officer, and the words made her wince.

Such behavior...

What behavior?

Two beautiful teenagers skinny-dipping, making love, laughing in a pool on one of the first mornings of real summer?

Even if they'd trespassed to do it, would Diana have wanted to have them arrested for such a crime?

Briefly she remembered the feel of cool water on her own naked skin, the way it had opened her body like an eye. And if she remembered correctly, *she'd* been trespassing... a neighbor's pool... heat rippling the air overhead... the sensation of floating outside her body, surrounded by dazzling white and blue.

She went upstairs, where she opened her closet. The skirts

and dresses and sweaters and blouses waited there, wearing their empty shapes and colors, the textures that had become familiar to her skin, the labels she'd squinted over the washing machine to read. Bodiless without her, or like souls without selves. Still, they exhaled the scent of her—her perfume and hair and skin. Diana pulled a summer dress off a hanger—a short white dress she hadn't worn since the year before—and quickly slipped off the sweat suit she'd put on that morning to drive her daughter to school.

She wasn't going to become *that* woman.

The one in the sweat suit, watching.

The one getting ready to call 9-1-1.

She remembered only too well what she herself had thought of *that* woman.

The sweat suit made a gray lump at her feet, and Diana kicked it into the bottom of her closet, then closed the closet door.

The hangers made discordant music knocking against one another.

Diana turned around with the white dress in her hands and looked at herself, naked, in front of the full-length mirror for a moment—she was still thin, her breasts were full and high, her legs and arms were thin and long, and her skin was still smooth—and she imagined herself swimming into the emptiness of that mirror, and the luminous emptiness of it smoothing against her flesh.

One of the girls keeps the spring 2000 Abercrombie and Fitch catalog on the nightstand next to her bed.

They look at it together, sitting on the floor with their backs against the twin bed. The metal bar of the bed frame is solid and cold against their spines, but it doesn't hurt. Both girls are so young, so healthy, so well fed . . . their bodies are so new to the world, blooming in it, that they've never felt stiff, never had aches, the kind that come from sitting in the wrong position for a long time, or lifting a heavy box without bending at the knees . . . the kinds of aches their mothers complain of, take Tylenol for, lie prone with for whole weekends on the couch while their daughters step quickly and lightly out of the thin doors, which close with the sound of an exhalation when they leave, aware of their own teenage bodies as only the vaguest sensations of pleasure . . . like new dresses made of silk, chiffon, or tulle, dresses that merely decorate the soul during its passage through the physical world.

With their spines pressed into that metal bar, they prop the catalog up between them, on their knees.

They aren't looking at the clothes, which are all the same; they're looking at the bodies of the models wearing the clothes, falling out of the clothes, shedding the clothes at the lakeshore, being pulled out of their clothes during muddy games of touch football.

Even on the cover of the catalog, the clothes don't matter. A teenage boy is rising naked out of a lake. If he's wearing clothes at all, they're below his waist.

The image burns itself into both girls' brains.

The flesh, the muscles, the water splashing between the boy, the camera, and them.

Inside the catalog, there are more bodies. All of them are perfect, and the clothes on them are unimportant. It's the torso, the arm, the breast that can be glimpsed inside the T-shirt or emerging from it that matters.

The clothes are ripped.

The clothes are dirty.

The clothes are unremarkable in every way, except that the perfection of the young bodies becomes even more apparent emerging from those clothes.

If it will ever seem alien to them—health, youth, beauty—neither of them can imagine it now, looking at the images in that two hundred-page advertisement for the physical world.

WEARING HER WHITE DRESS, WHICH SEEMED A BIT tighter than it had last summer, Diana went to Emma's room to make her daughter's bed.

She started with the bottom sheet, which she straightened and then attempted to tuck more snugly under the mattress. She hated fitted sheets. The corners were always snapping free. She lifted the mattress a little, and the elastic edge of the opposite end escaped from its place, just as she'd known it would.

Diana sighed, went to the other end of the mattress, and pulled the fitted sheet tight across it, then tried to tuck the elastic corner under, but then the *other* end of the sheet snapped loose.

It was a terrible game—the kind of game you might be forced to play in hell. In a hell for housewives, whores, or wayward girls . . . a game called Frustration or Wrestling with the Angel. Diana took a deep breath and felt her ribs strain against the waist of her white dress. Why was the dress tighter? The scale hadn't registered a single pound of new weight. Was her body simply shifting her weight around from one place to another?

She went back to the other end of the bed to try again.

When the bottom sheet was finally secured, she pulled the

top sheet and the comforter, with its little pink butterflies hovering in a pink sky, over the bed and tucked everything in. It was the way Emma liked her bed. Everything tucked.

Diana fluffed the pillows and lay them one on top of the other at the head of the bed, then picked Brownie and Pooh and Teddy off the floor, where they'd fallen in the night, and tossed them back on the bed. Then she leaned over to straighten them because they'd fallen awkwardly against one another, lifeless limbs flopping sloppily. With her back turned to her daughter's doorway, leaning over the bed, Diana thought for just a moment that she'd heard someone behind her, in the hallway, and she turned around quickly. No one was there.

Still there was a constriction in her chest—surprise? The dress? She realized that her head still hurt. Could it still be the headache from the night before? The cold juice in her daughter's cup? The struggle with the fitted sheet?

It was those things, she knew, but it was also those teenagers....

Though she hated to admit it to herself, she was still upset about them, and the headache and the fitted sheet and the teenagers making love in her neighbors' pool—it was the same to her. She felt as if she'd been defied by the very morning, the very *life,* she'd been determined to enjoy. The summer, the dusky leftovers of storm in the air, the quiet virtuality of her home with no one in it but herself...all of it made of matter, but the matter made of silence, of dreaming.

These mornings alone in her dream home, often Diana felt as if her hand could pass right through the furniture and walls.

All of it humming. All of it made out of shadow and light.

But this morning Diana had become distracted by her annoyance and annoyed by her distraction, as if she'd been wakened from a beautiful dream by the buzzing of a fly, and it had turned the beds and the curtains blowing in the breeze into mere artifacts, necessities. It had turned the morning into a chore.

Those teenagers. The nakedness. The fearlessness. The *audacity*.

Had she ever been bothered by the *audacity* of teenagers before?

Never.

She remembered well that she'd once been a teenager herself, that on more than one occasion the police had been called, warnings had been given. Once, she'd been parked with a boy—she could hardly have called him a boyfriend since she'd known him only a couple of days—in the empty parking lot of a strip mall on the outskirts of town.

Though Diana had forgotten that boy's name and his face, she could still recall the eerie fizz of the neon sign sputtering over the closed Laundromat. A static green. The car heater had been on because it was November, and the radio, which was playing loudly—rap music, the bass so thick and loud it was as if the car were its own big heart and they were inside its pumping.

Apparently someone had reported suspicious activity.

The boy and Diana were naked when the officer shone his flashlight into the backseat and ordered the boy to get his license out of his wallet.

While the boy was looking for the wallet in his pants' pocket, the cop made Diana step out of the car.

It couldn't have been more than forty degrees that night.

Diana could see the officer's hot breath escaping from him in smoky veils.

She tried to grab her black down jacket to hold in front of her, but the cop told her not to touch anything. He made her stand there, shivering, with her feet burning on the cold asphalt, and he looked at her while the boy in the car searched for his driver's license. He kept the frozen zero of his flashlight trained on her naked body, and moved it around. A cold eye.

She could remember the way she consciously removed her mind from the body he was looking at... removed her *self.* She let the other thing she knew she was—the part that could disengage itself from the legs and the breasts and the shivering—escape through an open space at the base of her brain, and Diana could imagine the look it caused to cross her face, the expression that made the policeman angry, made him sneer at her and shake his head. She'd seen the look on plenty of teenage girls' faces since then—*fuck you, go to hell, eat shit...*

The audacity. That's what it was.

Diana went back into her own bedroom and was surprised to see that the bed she shared with Paul had already been made.

When had she made it?

Before or after she'd changed her clothes?

And if she hadn't, when had *he*?

Had she simply not noticed that the bed was already made?

No... vaguely, she remembered tossing the pillows back onto the straightened quilt, which was a beautiful hand-stitched teal blue antique she'd bought at a flea market back before she'd become pregnant with Emma, the quilt under which she and Paul had been making love when Emma was conceived.

She remembered tossing the pillows into their places, but she could have sworn that was yesterday.

Or even the day before.

Diana stood looking at the bed, a little amused:

This is what happens, she thought, *with middle age.* Each day, if you were lucky, smoothed so effortlessly into the next that you couldn't tell one from the other. Life *went on*... and on and on and on. But no one knew this until he or she turned forty. Until then life was struggle and change—she remembered growing beans in Dixie cups in elementary school, an experiment, and the slow pale green eruption of the dirt, the bent necks, the wetness—and then suddenly that was over. From one stage to the next, until middle age, it had seemed as if one life ended and another took its place. Puberty, maturation, mating, marriage, pregnancy, baby—but then the stages blended into a sameness. A maintenance. Middle age. It was a river. A river you stepped into over and over again, finding it always the same.

It was a good time, Diana thought. It was the first time in her life she'd felt that the world was predictable, that her life was going to last, that what would happen the day after tomorrow could be predicted based on what had happened today.

Only in the last year had she begun to think of herself as *middle-aged.*

But maybe she wasn't middle-aged yet. It seemed to her that middle age was being pushed further and further back. Many of her friends and colleagues were older than she was and hadn't even had babies yet. One had just married the summer before and had worn a white wedding gown with a twelve-foot train. Her bridesmaids had worn light green chiffon and giggled like girls, though they were in their late thirties, at least.

It was a wonderful era in which to be middle-aged, if that's what she was. So many others, and everyone so fit, so healthy. Just the day before, she'd seen a photograph of a famous model (Christie Brinkley? Cindy Crawford?) on the cover of a magazine by the checkout line:

"Sexy at Sixty" the caption under her stunningly line-free face had read.

Perhaps it was airbrushing, but still . . . Diana was only forty, and here was this woman, who'd been beautiful and famous as long as Diana could remember, not seeming the least bit daunted by sixty.

Immortal. Undaunted. *Audacious.*

When Diana had been the age of those kids swimming naked in the Ellsworths' swimming pool, she would not have believed it. Forty would have been old. Forty might as well have been sixty, which might as well have been dead, no matter how well they could have fixed you up for a photograph. As a teenager Diana had known perfectly well what immortality was and that becoming middle-aged wasn't part of it.

But what had she *really* known then?

Then, she'd had no idea that she might someday look at herself in a mirror and be more than happy to overlook the lines around her eyes; the loose flesh at her belly button, where it had puckered like a kiss ever since she'd had the baby; the midriff (and that gold ring she used to wear through her navel!) she would no longer dream of exposing to the world, and be simply grateful that the gray in her hair was fairly easy, yet, to rinse away . . .

What would she have thought then if she had known that someday she'd be this woman in the mirror, the woman she was looking at now in a too-tight white dress, looking no older than forty, but definitely forty?

She looked more closely at herself in the mirror, and smiled.

She didn't have to teach that afternoon. She'd go to her studio and sketch for a while before she cleaned up the kitchen and living room. Perhaps, she thought whimsically, she'd come back in from her studio to find that she'd already vacuumed and dusted, too.

They put the Abercrombie and Fitch catalog back in its place on the nightstand, and they go to the kitchen.

The air-conditioning is on, and it fills the apartment with a false chill. Outside it's ninety degrees and nothing is moving, because there is no breeze. The tar in the streets has turned sticky. At the window where the air conditioner rattles, a stiff wind blows the curtains around as if there's an angry blizzard trying to escape.

"Want some ice cream?" one girl asks the other. She stands with the freezer open, and the cold ghosts drift in and around the Swanson dinners and the bags of mixed vegetables and the ice-cube bucket.

"Sure," the other says.

Bowls are taken out of the cupboard, spoons are tossed into the bowls, and a carton of Chocolate Silk ice cream is placed in the middle of the kitchen table.

They eat the dark sweetness until it's gone, and then they open a bag of Chee·tos that was sitting on top of the fridge.

"Want some diet Coke?"

They both laugh about that.

"Yeah," the other says, "I'm on a diet. Can't you tell?"

After the Chee·tos are almost gone, they make sandwiches from cold roast beef and American cheese, and eat them, and even after that they're still hungry.

They heat up a can of New England clam chowder.

They toss oyster crackers into the soup.

They finish with Chips Ahoy, right out of the bag.

Neither girl has ever been anything but slender and ravenous as long as she can remember—and will be slender and ravenous for as long as she can imagine.

THE TEENAGERS WHO'D BEEN IN THE POOL WERE GONE by the time Diana got to her studio loft above the garage.

If they'd still been there Diana would have had a bird's-eye view. And although that wasn't what she'd had in mind, she had to admit to herself she was a bit disappointed that they were now nowhere to be seen. Perhaps if they'd been lying in lawn chairs, poolside, Diana would have sketched their young and gleaming bodies. The girls' thick, wet hair. The boy's natural muscles. The unself-consciousness of those few humans who made perfectly beautiful nudes.

She'd been one once, and remembered what it was like to be flawless as a beam of light. . . .

Once, as a perfectly beautiful fifteen-year-old nude, she'd posed for a photographer—a man who must have been in his late forties, a stranger she'd met at the mall. He paid her sixty dollars to recline for an hour on the couch in his apartment—a couch he'd draped with a black satin sheet—while Diana's boyfriend paced around waiting for her in the man's smelly kitchen.

She and the boyfriend spent the money on a dinner at a steak house, and Diana could still remember the steak—a rib eye, medium rare—and the salad bar with its chilled ceramic bowls of bacon bits, crumbled hard-boiled egg, shredded cheddar cheese.

Her boyfriend was older. Nineteen. And Diana had never seen anyone eat as hungrily as he did that night, laughing between forkfuls about the old guy and his camera.

The photographer had claimed that he was going to sell the photos to a magazine, and Diana was flattered. She imagined her image reproduced glossily and sold at newsstands in big cities.

But Tony, her boyfriend, just kept laughing, saying the photographs hadn't been taken for any magazine. The old guy planned to keep them. He was probably developing them in his closet right now, jerking off.

It wasn't until then, in the restaurant with Tony laughing over his bloody steak and the bright iceberg lettuce littered with bacon bits, that Diana began to feel guilty. Stupid. Dirty.

They ordered dessert. Diana remembered that it had been called Mud Pie—chocolate ice cream on a dark, compressed pastry, drizzled with even darker chocolate. It had tasted, perhaps, as sweet and dense as the mud out of which God had fashioned the first human form...

Diana took out her box of charcoals and clipped a fresh sheet of paper to the easel and began to sketch the teenage bodies she'd seen—even though they were gone and she had always been best at drawing forms she could actually see. When she looked directly at the thing she was rendering, the process was easier, less inward. But when she drew from memory or imagination, there was often a sameness to the things she drew. The faces would be nearly identical every time—something about the eyes, even the eyes of old men, of children. They weren't exactly her own eyes she'd find herself giving those faces, but they were remembered eyes, *someone's* eyes, eyes that had imprinted themselves on her mind as the archetypal eyes, the eyes she saw watching her when she closed her own and imagined the *idea* of eyes.

Still she wanted to draw those kids, and the kids were gone, so Diana recalled what she could of them as she looked out her studio window at the Ellsworths' backyard. She sketched first what she saw—the lawn chairs, the pool, the sliding glass patio doors—and then she drew what she imagined:

The girl's figure, reclining in one of the chairs.

And then the boy, all sleekness and skin.

She drew the girl's arm, bent at the elbow, tossed casually over her head. It was a gesture Diana remembered making, a gesture that casually let the observer see the entirety of her nakedness.

With a charcoal shadow across her shoulder, Diana suggested that the body of the girl was wet. The boy's face was tilted toward the sky—chin lifted, arrogant. His eyes were closed.

The girl's legs were raised, crossed at the knee, as if she were swinging a foot.

Diana considered adding a cigarette to the hand bent above the girl's head. It seemed like something this girl might be doing, naked after sex in a stranger's pool, midmorning three weeks into June.

But she didn't do it. This girl didn't smoke.

She drew the girl's eyes last. Then she looked up from her drawing and out the window again to check the light. Would it be pouring over their heads—baptismal, cleansing? Or would it be slanted? Would the slanting elongate their forms, divest them of innocence, or—?

It was the light she was looking for—light's physical emptiness, as she described it to her students—as she parted the curtains again. Diana never worked in color. It was so much more interesting to see what could be done without it, the incredible range of what was possible to render with only darkness and light.

She'd been looking only for light, but there was movement down there. Something beyond the lime green leafiness of the trees.

It was the girl.

She'd come back.

She'd put on a white tank top and faded jeans, and she was bent over, buckling a high-heeled sandal. Her hair had dried, and it was gossamer blond. She looked up just at the moment that Diana looked down. Perhaps she'd seen the curtain move above her. . . .

Diana yanked it closed again, instinctively, and felt somehow embarrassed to have been looking out the window of her own studio.

Still she could see the girl through the sheerness of the curtain—although her form was muted, a shadow, nearly transparent. Perhaps stupidly Diana believed that the girl could no longer see *her*. But then the girl straightened herself, still looking toward the window.

She was a thin, tall girl.

She tucked a strand of pale blond hair behind her ear and rested all of her weight on one angular hip, then pulled the strap of her tank top up her shoulder. Still staring straight at the window, straight at Diana's face hiding behind the curtain there, the girl raised a middle finger from her fist and held it high.

Diana inhaled and took a fast step backward.

Her heart was racing.

She made her way to a chair in the corner of her studio and sat down.

Blood

Emma's pigtails had loosened, and in the sunlight several escaped strands of her golden hair shone like little filaments of light. She had her pink windbreaker tied around her waist, and Bethany Maria Anna Elizabeth under one arm. Her Snow White backpack was slung over the other arm, and it dragged along the ground beside her. When she opened the door of the minivan, she threw it all—the windbreaker, the backpack, and the doll—onto the floor.

Diana had never seen Bethany Maria Anna Elizabeth treated like an inanimate object before. Beneath the other things, with only her pale arm visible, the doll, to Diana, looked more like a human child than she'd ever seemed. A television image surfaced in her mind—an earthquake, a bombing?—of just such a child's arm emerging from the rubble.

Emma sat down next to Diana and pulled the minivan door

closed hard, and Diana leaned over the console to kiss her cheek.

It was hot, and Emma smelled like cafeteria—steam and soft carrots—though there *was* no cafeteria at Our Lady of Fatima. Emma took her own lunch with her to school every day, something sweet but nutritious that Diana had packed for her in a paper bag and put in her backpack.

The smell of cafeteria was Diana's own association with elementary school.

Hot lunch.

Some of the children at Diana's school had brought their own lunches in just the kind of paper bags Emma took hers in, but there was also hot lunch. Behind humid glass, in silver tubs, spooned up by an old woman wearing a hair net—spaghetti and green beans, hamburger patties and cooked carrots.

Diana's mother had always signed her up for that, but it was the mystery of those bagged lunches that Diana longed for. The peanut butter on bread that someone's mother had spread there herself. The stiff carrot sticks in plastic Baggies.

Emma was scowling, an expression that pulled her features downward and caused her to look like a woman, like *Diana,* instead of a child.

"Is something wrong, Emma?" Diana asked.

Emma said nothing. She turned her face away, but Diana could see the transparent reflection of it glaring at her in the window.

She backed up, looking carefully behind her, then pulled out of the semicircular drive.

As she pulled into the road, Diana was conscious of how smooth it was under her wheels, the sensation of floating inside two tons of machinery. Maybe they'd repaved this road. It was like driving on layers and layers of black silk, or the slick petals of black tulips, as if the road had been carpeted with them.

She glanced over at Emma again, but Emma still had her face turned to the window. She looked down at her daughter's knees, which were exposed between her kneesocks and her plaid skirt. They were dirty—a dry, dusty dirt—as if Emma had recently knelt in ashes.

Diana cleared her throat, preparing to invent for herself a firm but sensitive maternal tone.

"Emma," she said, "look at me."

Emma didn't look.

Diana could see the very pale place at the base of Emma's skull where her pigtails parted, and it made her feel frightened and protective. She reached out to touch her daughter's golden hair, but as soon as Emma felt her touch she flinched away.

Diana pulled her hand back.

She cleared her throat again.

"Emma," Diana said more sharply, "I told you to look at me."

Still Emma didn't move. Her face was turned resolutely, as if permanently, away from her mother.

Diana felt something moving just under her ribs.

What was it?

Anger? Panic?

Guilt?

It was a crawling sensation similar to the one she'd had when she was pregnant... something swimming inside her... something that wasn't violent, something that meant no harm but was kicking with all the strength it had.

Diana held more tightly to the steering wheel than she needed to and bit her lower lip. It was something she used to do when she was Emma's age—bite her lower lip until it bled. For years she'd had a scab there, which she could never keep from biting or fingering long enough to let it heal. It had driven her mother crazy, that scab. She'd slap at Diana's hand every time it went near her lip. She'd grab her chin and say, "Stop it!" whenever she caught Diana biting it, which was about a hundred times a day. Still Diana hadn't stopped until she was in seventh grade and a boy she liked pointed at the scab and said, "Gross. What's that?"

Diana inhaled. She reached over and patted the dark dust on her daughter's knees, but Emma moved away from the touch and pulled the plaid skirt down over the dirt.

Diana inhaled sharply and put her hand back on the steering wheel. "Young lady," she said, "you'd better tell me right this minute what's going on."

The outburst was a damp explosion. "No!" Emma screamed, burying her face in her hands. "You can't make me! You can't make me do *anything*."

Emma started thrashing so violently that Diana was afraid she might grab the door handle and throw herself out of the minivan. It wasn't until that moment that Diana noticed that Emma's seat belt wasn't buckled.

She reached across her daughter, who fought, thrashing, against her, for the silver buckle of the seat belt. It was cold as a little gun in her hand. She pulled it across Emma, but Emma reacted to this as if her mother were trying to put her in a straitjacket or slip a noose around her neck. She kicked at the glove compartment with the heel of her white canvas shoes until it finally snapped open and spilled its contents—a map, a tampon, an owner's manual—onto the pile of Emma's things that she'd thrown onto the floor.

Diana glanced down at the map, which had fallen open to

what looked like a limb—broken, veined, tangled with freeways and highways.

California.

The map had been in the glove compartment since their trip out West the summer before.

Diana let the seat belt's silver buckle slip from her hand, and she gripped the wheel tightly again, staring straight out the windshield, steering home....

Death Valley. She'd always remember that...

The long shadowless drive through its blond dust, and the eerie sense she'd had that she'd been there before. But who wouldn't feel that way? How many movies had been filmed there, and how many of them had Diana seen whether she remembered them or not?

It was a hundred and twenty degrees outside, but they'd had the air-conditioning on, and inside the minivan they were wearing sweaters. In the rearview mirror mounted at the passenger's side window (Paul was driving) Diana could see the Funeral Mountains sinking blackly into the desert behind them.

She'd loved Death Valley—the sweeping grandeur of it, the way even the most vivid imagination could not have invented it, not even come close. And as they traveled closer to the ocean, and California began to shift gradually into its moss green lushness, Diana had felt homesick for the endless, soulless expanse of what they'd left.

One of the girls has never had a boyfriend.

But years before, she had a vision of Jesus while she was sitting in a pew of the church to which her mother took her. Jesus was kneeling at the altar with his hands folded. His hair was reddish brown, and it hung down his back. He was wearing a torn white robe. The reason she knew it was Jesus was that he appeared out of nowhere and then became more and more translucent as she watched him until he disappeared.

Not long after that her mother quit taking her to that church. She didn't like that her daughter was spending so much time with the youth group. She walked into the basement of the church one Saturday afternoon to pick her up and found her with seven other teenagers weeping and clinging to one another on a gym mat on the floor. One of the older girls was speaking in tongues, and her eyes were rolled back in her head.

But lately she's begun thinking about boys. Her body is a bit too warm all the time. Nate Witt, or the boy with one arm at the Burger King, or some college boy she might meet downtown at the French Café...

But the other girl has not been a virgin for a very long time. She sees her soul as a little pinprick somewhere just above her stomach. Lately she's begun to think about sin. She's had dreams in which an elderly man with leathery skin stands above her bed and weighs her sins on a balance.

The good deeds are weightless, made of white Styrofoam chips, the kind they use to pack breakable things that need to be shipped.

But the sins are made of red and swollen fruit. They're overripe, and though there are as many good deeds as sins, the sins are so heavy that the scales tip right over and spill their contents onto the floor of her bedroom, and the old man laughs.

That girl wishes something would come to cleanse her, baptize her, empty and clean her body like a glass bottle.

"Let's go to Baskin Robbins," one of the girls says to the other.

They've spent the afternoon watching soap operas they've never seen before, guessing at what the conflicts and dilemmas of the characters must be. Though the air-conditioning is on full blast, it only cuts a path through the heat in the apartment.

"Mint chocolate chip!" the other girl says, sitting up straighter on the couch.

"French vanilla," the other says.

She points the remote control at the television, and the screen turns black.

DIANA WAS STILL TREMBLING AS SHE DROVE, BUT EMMA had grown quiet beside her, just the leftover hiccuping of her sobs.

Pulling the minivan into the driveway, Diana was relieved to see Paul in his usual spot on the front porch. He waved, as he always did, largely and generously, but Emma was still staring out the passenger window and Diana could only bring herself to lift a hand in his direction. The word *fool* flashed through her like some kind of airy bullet, in and out, without disturbing so much as an atom but leaving a sense of itself behind.

"Go to your room," she said to Emma gently but seriously, and Emma leaped out and ran into the back door of the house, leaving her windbreaker, backpack, and Bethany Maria Anna Elizabeth crumpled on the floor of the minivan along with the spilled contents of the glove compartment.

Diana heard the screen door close behind her daughter like a slap.

She had to hold her breath to squeeze out because she'd parked so close to the garage wall, and then she had to let her white dress press against the side of the minivan to get out of the garage, though she knew it would probably leave a shadow of dust and dirt against her hip. The darkness of the garage smelled of pine and rot when she inhaled again, and when she knocked over a rake it made a rattling and tinny sound that Diana felt in her teeth. She propped the rake back up against one of the exposed beams of the garage.

Her eyes watered when she stepped back out into the sun—those sunglasses, she still hadn't bought a pair—and she rubbed them as she walked toward the front of the house, where she knew Paul was waiting. She passed, as she had to, the daisies, which were staring straight into the sun without blinking. Some kind of pollen was hovering around them, and Diana could feel it in her throat and lungs, and she coughed.

Paul stood up when he saw her. He had his hands in the pockets of his khaki pants, and he was chewing on a corner of his mustache, looking worriedly from his brown shoes to Diana. She knew he'd seen that something was wrong, but rather than looking concerned or curious, he looked . . . what? Guilty? Fearful? Diana wasn't sure.

"Is everything okay?" Paul asked.

He was looking shyly at Diana, one shoulder raised as if (could it be?) he expected to be slapped, as if he were protecting his face.

Diana looked at him—the expression, the posture—for a moment before she spoke. Then she cleared her throat of the pollen—that sweet and poisonous flower dust—and said, "Something's wrong with Emma. She had . . . I don't know . . . a temper tantrum in the car."

Perhaps Paul looked relieved. In any case the shoulder dropped and he met Diana's eyes. He furrowed his brow, stroked his gray beard, and said like an actor comfortable with his lines, "I'll talk to her."

Diana nodded, still regarding him carefully. After so many years she still found him attractive. More than once while driving downtown near campus, maybe on her way to meet him for lunch, maybe on some other errand, she'd caught a glimpse of a man walking down the sidewalk, briefcase in one hand, the other tucked casually into his pants pocket, and she'd felt an instant tug of physical attraction, a desire to look more closely, before she realized who it was—the stranger she wanted to look at more closely was her husband.

The gray in his hair and beard hadn't changed anything. And he was still slim. His eyes were pale and blue—the mild eyes of a professor, though his features were chiseled. Ruggedly handsome, she liked to think. He had the face of a man who might have found himself in a younger incarnation out West—climbing mountains, white-water rafting, rustling cattle—if he hadn't been in graduate school.

Still, as he stepped through the front door of the house they shared, as Diana watched him cross the threshold into the dream house they'd shared for fifteen years, she heard it again...

Fool.

She almost looked over her shoulder to see where the word had come from.

The daisies?

The lawn?

It had come from outside of herself. She touched the side of her face, feeling a bit dizzy, but then the dizziness passed and she was left with nothing but the sensation of having been spoken to by someone she couldn't see.

Only once in her life, more than two decades before, had

she heard a voice in the way she imagined people *heard voices.* And it had terrified her then, because the voice—as with this word—had been so clear. It had seemed to come from beyond her, entering her mind from her *ear*... a girl's voice, hollow and familiar—though all it had said was her name:

Diana.

She was fifteen at the time, lying in her lover's bed. He'd taken her that afternoon to a clinic downtown where she'd had an abortion. The clinic had been very clean. It smelled like floral-scented tissues. There were pastel watercolors on the walls and flutey music piped in from the ceiling. She'd been nauseated for weeks, and the paintings and the music made the back of her neck trickle with cold sweat.

Her lover, Marcus, held her hand in the waiting room. He had rough hands, the backs of which were covered with coarse black hair, and those hands in that room full of flute and pale pink flowers and sails had seemed obscenely out of place. They had seemed to be the reason for her nausea, that this masculine ugliness had entered and taken root inside her. She wanted it out. It never crossed her mind for one minute to have a baby, or that what had happened to her could possibly end in motherhood.

She let Marcus hold her hand, but she hated it, hated him, vowed that after this was over and he'd paid the receptionist for what they were going to do to her, she would never speak to him again.

Marcus was in his thirties. He kept exotic pets in his aluminum-sided house at the end of a street in a bad neighborhood outside of Briar Hill—a lynx in the garage, a panther in a cage behind his house. He had a dog, too, that lived peacefully enough inside, lapping up water and dog food right under the kitchen table, but that dog was almost pure wolf. Its eyes were icy. Sometimes for no apparent reason the dog would lift its head to the water-stained ceiling tile in the bedroom, while Marcus and Diana made love, and howl—a sound full of primitive warning and horror.

"She's harmless," Marcus always said.

But he also said this of the panther, who would throw itself snarling against the bars of its cage when Diana so much as looked in its direction. Its teeth were so white against its blackness that they seemed to be made of light.

The lynx, however, she had only glimpsed through the window of the garage. It was leashed to a beam, and it was pacing, head down, back and forth, back and forth, though Diana could see the crazy tufts of hair near its ears that made it look like no cat she'd ever seen.

A devil cat.

A cat that had risen from its ninth life terribly altered.

Marcus himself had piercingly blue eyes. They were gorgeous eyes and always made more dazzling by the blue work shirts he wore and by the black stubble of his beard against his pale skin. She'd met him at a party, where he was selling marijuana to some boys she knew. After the first time they made love, Marcus said, "I like young girls, but you're the only one I've ever met who isn't afraid."

It had never occurred to her to be afraid.

Marcus was the one who'd given Diana Timmy, the cat. Timmy, who lived to be twenty and slept at the foot of Diana's bed for years after Marcus was only the vaguest memory of a beast's hand.

The procedure had been quick, and the only pain had been a dull cramping, and afterward, when they helped her up from the paper-covered table she'd been lying on, she realized that the nausea was gone. It was as if it had been wiped away with a washcloth. She was so relieved, she wept.

But afterward, the bleeding went on and on.

The blood was thick and clotted, and when they called the clinic to ask them if this much bleeding was normal, they had said it probably was, and to lie down, and if it got worse to go straight to the emergency room.

Diana lay down in Marcus's bed. The ceiling above her was cracked right down the middle, and she stared at the crack, imagining herself slipping into it, disappearing.

Marcus went to the kitchen to get her a glass of water, and that's when she heard it.

The voice.

Right up close to her ear.

So close she could feel the breath of it enter her with the word...

Diana.

She sat up in bed, gasping, just as Marcus came back with a coffee cup full of water for her.

"What's wrong?" he asked.

"Nothing," she said.

"Should we go to the emergency room now?"

Diana just shook her head and lay back down.

Eventually the bleeding stopped, but by then Marcus's sheets had been soaked with it. Before he drove her back to her mother's apartment, Marcus had asked her sheepishly if she could please clean it up. He didn't think he could do it himself. He felt very squeamish about blood.

Marcus, with his wild animals.

Marcus, with his hairy hands.

Diana had torn the sheets off the bed and stuffed them into the trash bag for him, and he'd been pathetically grateful to her for it.

Fool.

She followed Paul into the house.

The ice cream is heavy with cold sweetness. It takes the boy behind the glass counter a long time to dig it up with his silver scoop. He's a thin boy, maybe seventeen, with a red rash and a purple-black hickey on his neck.

Mint chocolate chip in a cup. Vanilla in a sugar cone. They pay him and take their ice cream outside, where they sit on a bench under a tree at the edge of the sidewalk.

On a bench across from theirs, a little girl is sitting so close to her father it looks as if the two of them are glued to each other. The father is young and handsome, and his daughter has blond pigtails. She's taking tiny nibbles of the blue ice cream in her cone while the father looks at her admiringly, urging her on, his eyes narrowed in the bright light of the summer afternoon and his own adoration.

The little girl's attention is entirely on her Blue Moon, but her father's physical presence beside her does not seem taken for granted. When he shifts his weight on the bench and his body moves centimeters from hers, the little girl scoots over until she is securely next to him again.

The ice cream is dense but formless. It has no center, no structure, no bones. Its sweetness slips into them easily, and before long it's gone. They rise from the bench and start the walk home, passing on their way the little girl, whose Blue Moon has begun to melt and is dripping onto her father's jeans in bright splashes. He hasn't noticed.

AFTER PAUL HAD GONE UPSTAIRS TO SPEAK TO EMMA, Diana went to the kitchen and looked in the freezer. . . .

Maybe she would simply make hamburgers for dinner. It was something Emma usually liked. And frozen French fries. Lots of ketchup in a puddle on her plate.

But what Diana really had a craving for was steak.

A bloody one.

Charbroiled.

The taste of carbon and salt. A rib eye, or a T-bone.

But she'd have had to go to the grocery store, and it was getting too late now. She was, she realized, hungry. Famished. They'd have to eat soon.

Diana took the hamburger out of the meat drawer in the refrigerator. It was fresh in its shrink-wrapped package. Very red, though flecked with fat. She cut a slit in the package with a sharp knife and peeled the edges away.

The smell of it was sweet. It made her mouth water.

She set the package on the Formica countertop and pulled the plastic bag of frozen fries out of the freezer, then turned the broiler on and shook the fries onto a cookie sheet.

They were stiff, furred with frost, and the cold of them burned her hand as she spread them out on the sheet. Then she took the skillet down from where she kept it on a hook over the stove and turned on the gas.

The blue bracelet sputtered up from the place where it had been waiting.

The hamburger was cold between her palms, though not as cold as the fries had been, as she clapped it into patties. It left a waxy film on her hands... the fat; it was always hard to wash away. She'd have to rub her hands under hot water and scrub with soap.

When the pan was hot Diana slapped all but one of the four hamburger patties (two for Paul) into the skillet. There was the usual angry sizzle when the raw meat hit the hot cast iron.

The pattie she hadn't tossed into the pan, she picked up. She brought it close to her nose, and breathed it in....

Diana could hardly ever remember being so hungry, so hungry that this raw meat seemed too delicious, too tempting, not to taste.

She knew it wasn't a healthy thing, eating raw meat....

Bacteria. Parasites. Mad Cow Disease.

But the meat was so fresh. She knew there were restaurants where they served raw beef, countries in which it was a delicacy. How much different than sushi, which Diana loved and ate frequently, could it be?

She tasted just the edge.

It was even better than she'd imagined.

Cold and delicate.

If not for the tangy rust of blood, it would have been almost tasteless.

She considered salting it but thought then that it was precisely this vagueness, this mildness, that made the taste so satisfying. That and the texture, which was as smooth as anything she'd ever eaten. As smooth as pudding, as smooth as ice cream or guacamole, but so much denser. This was, after all, the smoothness of flesh. Before she heard Emma and Paul on the stairs, she'd eaten all of it.

Part Three

Silence

"Aren't you having a hamburger?" Paul asked.

They were sitting around the dining room table as they always did, though Emma wouldn't look up from her plate.

"I already ate," Diana said, and shrugged, "while you were upstairs. I was famished. I'll just have fries."

She looked from Paul to Emma, then raised her eyebrows . . . a question.

Paul just shrugged, shook his head, and raised his shoulders . . . an answer.

They could have communicated with one another this way forever, Diana thought, and the idea of that pleased her. The idea of marriage. Of the level of intimacy she shared with her husband, a level at which there was no need for language.

Her own parents had never had it. They'd stayed married for ten years, but they'd never seemed married, to Diana. She was eight when they separated, but the word *separate* already defined them. She had almost no childhood memories of her mother and father in a room together. They ate at different hours, watched different television shows in different rooms in the evenings. They slept in the same bed, but asleep in it they might as well have been on different continents, drifting—his was a hot steamy continent, hers was sanded clean by a cool breeze.

It wasn't until much later, when Diana began to get in trouble and her parents had been divorced for years, that they seemed to meet somewhere in the middle of a bridge. The bridge of parenthood. She could still remember the strange warmth that spread through her chest when she saw her mother, weeping, throw herself into her father's arms at the police station one blue-black winter morning, and the calm familiarity with which her father had patted her mother's back.

They'd created her, that embrace seemed to say.

If it hadn't been for the two of them, despite how much they'd grown to dislike one another, where would she have been? Who?

That embrace admitted it:

She *wouldn't* have been.

But the warmth of that embrace turned cold when it hit the air. Her mother had picked her father up to bring him to the police station because his car was in the shop, and when she pressed him for details about his car trouble, he grew silent and slouched in the passenger seat. Then they began to bicker about Diana, who was slouched behind them just as her father was slouched beside her mother—chastened, hoping only that the subject at hand would pass. As they snapped at one another about what to do concerning their daughter and who deserved the blame, Diana watched Briar Hill slip around outside the car window.

Briar Hill, with its quaint clapboard houses and brick facades.

It was like a stage set, not a hometown.

The rolling lawn of the university commons was deserted, and the thin layer of snow coating it glowed a fiery pink in the sun coming up. She felt loathing for it—the lawn, the snow, the university where her mother worked as a secretary ("administrative assistant" they called it) in the philosophy department.

She felt hatred for the smug, clean students—none of whom were out this early, but whose ghosts she could see moving from class to class in their down jackets... the students to whom her father, for a living, sold stereo equipment.

She hated the professors, who were either men with beards or women in flat shoes and knee-length skirts.

She hated Briar Hill.

The prettiness, the peace, the *decentness* of the place. She thought of the little village scene set up in the window of the gift shop at Christmas. The miniature train running in circles around it. The fake snow. The little fires painted inside the ceramic houses. A hammer smashing it to chalky bits.

She'd ended up at the police station that night because she'd disturbed the peace of Briar Hill by arguing loudly with her boyfriend outside his parents' house, which was one of those clapboards—bric-a-brac, front porch with a scrolled railing.

His parents were off at some conference in Chicago, and she and the boy had been smoking dope and staring at the aquarium in his parents' living room. His father propagated corals as a hobby, and although at first the corals seemed merely to be decorations to Diana, no more interesting than the dried flower arrangements scattered throughout the house, after a few minutes of watching them she realized that they *weren't* decorations.

They were *alive,* like animals, like brains. Inside them the whole world was being dreamed, and she was a part of the dream.

She could see the image of herself in the aquarium glass and realized entirely, and for the first time, that *she* was the one who was a decoration. *She* could be *seen through.* A hand could have passed straight through her, waved her image away, waved her out of the world altogether.

But the corals... they were heavier than she was. More solid. Heavy with thought. Breathing in the underwater blue.

If she didn't disturb them, maybe they would let her stay.

She stayed for a while lost among them, stoned, staring... a thought swimming between pulsing minds. The one with the blue fingers. The one with the little stars at the end of each strand of hair. The one like a small pink shrub, the branches of it made of flesh. But when she turned to look at Brian, whom she'd met at Big Mama's CDs & Tapes and only known for a few days (they hadn't even kissed yet, though she knew they would, that they'd end up fucking, that it was why he'd invited her to his parents' house while they were out of town)... when she turned to look at him to see if he understood, if he was with her, speechless, among the other life-forms, she saw that he'd unzipped his pants, that he was staring at the side of her face, not at his father's corals, and that he was stroking his erection.

When she looked down at it he grabbed her hand and tried to replace his own with hers, and yanked her out of the most beautiful vision she'd ever had, the closest she'd ever come to understanding... what?

Now she'd never know, and she slapped him. "Fuck you!" she screamed.

At first he laughed, but when Diana tried to stand up, to get away, he pushed her back onto the couch.

She fought it—punching, kicking. It wasn't the sex she was fighting against—she'd expected the sex—but it was the return to the world, which seemed even uglier and more vulgar than it had since she'd been away.

He ripped her blouse. He called her a slut. She told him she had an older lover with a panther who'd come and kick his ass.

He slapped her, hard.

They knocked over a lamp.

She tasted blood on her tongue and spit at him. Then she ran out the front door, with no shoes on, and the frost felt like shards of glass under her feet. He knocked her to the ground, and she scratched his face. He knocked her head against the lawn, but even with the frost, the grass was soft. She kicked him in the balls. When the police pulled in the driveway, they stopped.

One of the girls gets her driver's license, and now she can have the car all day if she drops her mother off at work at nine o'clock in the morning and is there to pick her up at five.

"Let's just drive around," she says.

She turns the radio on. They're playing a song that was popular a decade ago. It sounds computerized and reminds the girls of sitting in the backseats of their mothers' cars, eating Pop-Tarts, being driven to elementary school.

They sing along.

They roll down their windows.

They stop at a red light beside a car idling in the left-turn lane.

In that car, there are also two teenage girls—one dark, one light. They're smoking and listening to the very same song on the same radio station.

They look over. They wave and laugh.

When the light changes, the two cars full of music and girls go their separate ways.

The roads, the world, the summer... they're full of teenage girls driving and singing.

"Why don't *we* smoke?" one girl asks the other loudly over the music.

"Because it's disgusting," the other answers.

EMMA ATE HER HAMBURGER IN NIBBLES, PUTTING IT DOWN every few bites to take a sip of milk, swipe a fry through ketchup, then eat it.

She was almost done with her dinner when the phone rang.

Diana raised her eyebrows to Paul. The expression meant *Should we answer that or let the machine get it?*

He lifted his eyes toward the ceiling, considering, then looked at her. It meant *Who could that be? Maybe we ought to get it.*

Diana got to the phone just as the answering machine picked up, which meant that she had to shout, "Hello? Hold on a minute..." over her own voice, which was saying, as if to contradict her, "We aren't available to take your call right now..."

Diana fumbled with a few different buttons until she hit the right one and cut herself off in midsentence.

"Mrs. McFee?"

"Yes?" Diana asked.

"This is Sister Beatrice."

"Oh, Sister Beatrice," Diana said, trying to sound pleasantly surprised.

"I was hoping you could come in tomorrow morning before school. Something has arisen with Emma."

"Oh," Diana said. She felt a quick funnel of air whirl around her face. She said, "I'd be happy to come in, but what seems to be the problem?"

Sister Beatrice cleared her throat, then said, "Did Emma show you a copy of the story she brought to school today?"

"Yes, I—"

"She *did*?" Sister Beatrice's astonished tone sounded phony, or was it gleeful? "Then you must know what the problem is—"

"I'm sorry?" Diana asked. "There was some problem with the story?"

"Excuse me," Sister Beatrice said, "I think if you'd seen the story you'd understand the problem. I made a copy of it, but I returned the original to Emma. I think she put it in her backpack. I told her she'd better show it to her parents when she got home."

"I guess I haven't—" Diana cut herself off. She touched her forehead and was surprised to find it beaded with cold sweat.

"Well, as I said, I have a copy here if she didn't bring it home—"

"If you told her to bring it home, I'm sure she did," Diana said. "I'll find—"

"Good," Sister Beatrice said. "And I'll see you then tomorrow morning? Is seven forty-five too early?"

"No," Diana said. "I'll see you in the morning, Sister."

"Good-bye," Sister Beatrice said as if she weren't quite ready to hang up, but Diana put the receiver back into its place quickly.

"Emma," Diana said softly when she stepped back into the dining room.

Emma was swirling a French fry around and around in a tiny puddle of ketchup.

"Emma. Do you know who that was?"

"No," Emma snapped. She looked straight up at Diana defiantly. Paul looked from Emma to Diana.

"That was Sister Beatrice."

Diana felt strangely afraid. . . .

Afraid of Emma, afraid of Sister Beatrice, afraid of what had happened and might happen next. It was a fear completely out of proportion to the events, but her life, for so long now, had been so simple, so free of . . .

She had no idea, now, what she'd do if trouble . . .

"So?" Emma asked.

Her daughter's voice startled her. It was, she realized, her own younger voice.

Her own younger voice come back to haunt her.

"So," Diana said, trying to sound calm. "So, go out to the car and get your backpack."

Emma said nothing. She slid from her chair and stomped out.

"What's this all about?" Paul asked.

Diana shrugged, but she felt defensive. She felt that Paul was looking at her too closely, as if he could see past her eyes into her mind, past her mind into *her*.

She shrugged and looked away from him. She said, "Sister

Beatrice said she wanted to see me in the morning. Something about a story Emma wrote."

Paul nodded. He said, "That's what Emma said when I asked her what was the matter. She said she was upset because of a story, but she said that *you* wrote the story."

The screen door slammed weakly.

"Here," Emma said, shoving a piece of paper, which was folded into fourths, at her mother, then she ran up the stairs.

Diana took the paper and carefully unfolded it.

Paul looked over her shoulder.

> *Bethany Maria Anna Elizabeth is very naughty. She wants to show boys her underpants. She is a bad dirty girl. Who should I kill? Who should I kill? Kill Bethany Maria Anna Elizabeth, not me.*

Skin

"I *HAVE* NO EXPLANATION FOR IT," DIANA SAID.

Sister Beatrice looked at her blankly. The eyes behind her wire-rimmed glasses were so pale they appeared nearly white . . . the eyes of a snowy owl, Diana thought, or some color-blind creature, some bird or animal that spent most of its life staring into frozen waste, waiting for the shadow of something small and mammalian to move.

Sister Beatrice looked from Diana to the piece of paper between them, then reached out and folded it back along the original lines into which it had been folded, as if she could no longer bear to look at it.

Diana had thought that the days of nuns in habits were over, that the nuns of this generation simply wore skirts and blouses and sensible shoes. She wasn't entirely sure she'd have opted to send her daughter to a Catholic girls' school if she'd seen Sister Beatrice before enrolling Emma.

The habit Sister Beatrice wore was starched stiff, though it still managed to fall in sharp folds around her. Only her small pale hands and her powder white face could be glimpsed underneath it all. If Sister Beatrice had hair or breasts or voluptuous hips, it wasn't possible to see them, or even to imagine them. The illusion was of sexlessness, *bodilessness.*

Sister Beatrice was ageless as well. Sitting across the desk from her and looking closely, Diana could see that her face was unlined. The skin on her cheekbones looked thin, tissuey, but there were no wrinkles around her eyes. Her eyebrows were pencil thin and black.

"As I said," Diana tried to explain, but now she was trembling and there was a cold chill rising from the hard wooden chair she was sitting in and from the linoleum under that, which was flecked with gold. "As I said, this couldn't be Emma's doing, because she doesn't know how to use my husband's computer. She's never even turned it on by herself, and"—Diana put her palms up empty on the table between them—"I'm sure you know as well as I do that this is nothing like Emma. This is just not the kind of thing Emma would ever do."

Diana put her hand over the piece of paper, folded into fourths, as if to keep Sister Beatrice from picking it up again. *Guilt.* She knew she had the look and smell of it about her. She felt it under her skin like a hot and slippery lining. But she *had not; why would she?*

And if not her, then who? And why? And how had they managed to snatch the original story from Emma's Snow White backpack and replace it with this ugly thing, this story twisted out of Emma's sweet and innocent original, perverted?

Briefly it crossed Diana's mind that the only person besides herself who could have done it, who could have switched the pieces of white paper, who would have known where to find the first one and where to stash the second, was Sister Beatrice herself.

At that moment, the nun looked up from Diana's hand to her face. It was as if she were trying to see through her. *You can't,* Diana wanted to say, *I'm made of flesh and blood.* But Sister Beatrice stared through her anyway. Sister Beatrice knew something; Sister Beatrice *saw* something and didn't like it. . . .

It was the only explanation—though it was also no explanation at all.

Sister Beatrice stood up and said, "We can bring Emma in now."

Diana stood up, too, but her chair made a terrible scraping sound as she did, and it felt as if the sound had pierced her. She put her hand to her head. *Headache,* she thought, and had to steady herself with a few fingers at the edge of Sister Beatrice's steel desk. Sister Beatrice went to the classroom door and opened it and called into the silent hallway for Emma, who'd been waiting out there.

Diana could feel the blood pumping at her temple. She kept her fingers on that pulse to try to hold off the headache she felt coming. When she glanced up she looked directly into the eyes of the Virgin Mary, whose portrait was hanging above the perfectly blank chalkboard.

The Virgin Mary was holding her own heart in her hands. It was pierced with a dagger. The dagger was exactly like the sound Diana's chair had made when she stood up, scraping itself across the linoleum. She felt sick, dizzy, and had to sit back down, and when she did, the denim skirt she was wearing crept up her thighs, and the Virgin Mary seemed to regard this as if it were something that disappointed but did not surprise her. Her expression didn't change. It was as if she had been waiting.

Diana tried to wrestle the skirt back down over her thighs and wished she'd thought to wear a longer skirt—and pantyhose. The weather had been so warm and fresh in the morning that she didn't think twice about putting on the skirt, which she'd owned since she was in college.

But waiting for her daughter to return with the nun, with the Virgin Mary regarding her casually, Diana questioned her own motives. It seemed to her now that the clothing she'd chosen to wear had been meant to provoke something... someone.

But who?

The Virgin Mary?

Sister Beatrice?

It *had* pleased and surprised Diana that morning to see how well the skirt still fit, and that her legs looked polished and perfect. The janitor had looked them over slowly when she entered Our Lady of Fatima with her daughter at 7:45. And Sister Beatrice had glanced at them, too, her lips a thin white line.

Diana sat at the very edge of the child-sized chair she'd been given to sit in, and managed to pull the skirt about halfway down her thighs.

When Emma came back into the classroom, she was followed by Sister Beatrice, who straightened the collar of Emma's white blouse as if *she* were Emma's mother—though she did not look maternal. She looked like a crow that had mothered a little girl.

Neither Emma nor Sister Beatrice looked at Diana. They both had their eyes turned toward the Virgin Mary—or was it the blackboard, or the clock above the blackboard, ticking and institutional, with a red second hand that seemed to be moving too fast?

Sister Beatrice said to Emma, "We're going to drop this matter, Emma. Often there's no explanation for evil, and no way to locate its source."

They drive until they've gotten to the outskirts of Briar Hill.

There the subdivisions melt into swamp; the swamps turn to cornfields. There are pastures full of sheep who stand stone still, staring at the ground. Some of the sheep have been sheared, and they have stripes and *X*s of blood on them.

The girls pass a country church. It's all red brick and stained glass like a church out of an old book, with a cemetery behind it, circled by a black wrought-iron fence. The gate, with its black sword tips, is open.

"Let's go read the stones," one of them says. It's something she used to do with her mother, who'd studied literature in Scotland for a few years before she married her father and became a secretary in the philosophy department. But her mother had still liked old things, maudlin and haunted things, and sometimes she'd take her daughter to some of the older cemeteries in Briar Hill—the ones where the people were buried whose names were the names of streets and buildings now—and they'd wander among the graves.

The girls park in the shade of the steeple, which is sharp and white with a dangerous-looking cross at the top, and they pass through the gate.

Both are wearing shorts and summer tops with spaghetti straps. No bras. One of them wears her shorts low enough that the rose tattooed on her hip shows. They have dark eyeshadow on, and deep-mauve lipstick, and their skin is very white because they never go into the sun without sunscreen on. They've seen the effects of the sun on the faces of their mothers, and it won't happen to them.

Under the girls' feet, the farmers and the German immigrants and their wives and children are bones and teeth in boxes.

Neither girl has ever spent much time in the country. Never gone camping or spent the summer on a farm...

The dead in this country churchyard could not have imagined these girls any better than these girls can imagine the dead.

IT WAS A WINDY MORNING.

The sky was full of purple clouds, which scuttled quickly overhead. Perhaps it would rain. Perhaps this would be the first afternoon thunderstorm of the summer. Perhaps it was tornado weather.

Better today than tomorrow, Diana thought, when the third grade would be going to the zoo for their last day of school.

The wind had blown a few light branches out of the trees, and they littered the neighborhood. When Diana ran over them in the minivan, they snapped like skinny bones.

Emma had seemed happy when Diana kissed her good-bye in the classroom. Sister Beatrice had watched them part, and her shadow fell between them. Still, Diana's headache had passed before it even started, seeing her daughter smile.

Emma *had* been smiling, and even before Sister Beatrice offered her exoneration, Emma had seemed back to normal... a girl much more worried about her pigtails than her soul. Emma had known that Diana was meeting with Sister Beatrice, but both Diana and Paul had reassured her that they knew there'd been some kind of mistake.

"You'll tell her I didn't write the story?" Emma asked.

"Of course, honey," Paul had said. "You said you didn't write it, and we believe you."

"I swear it," Emma said. "I swear it on my life."

Emma had thrown herself into Paul's arms, and he'd looked at Diana over his daughter's shoulder.

Diana couldn't tell, this time, what the look conveyed.

Did he blame Diana?

Did he think, somehow, that Diana had, as Emma originally believed, written the story *herself,* slipped it into Emma's backpack, set her own daughter up for . . . for what?

And why in god's name would Diana have done such a thing?

"Of course," Diana reassured Emma. She had the story, folded in fourths, in her hand like a permission slip, a doctor's excuse, an indulgence.

But again . . . for what?

"Of course I'll tell her there was some terrible mistake," Diana said to Emma, "that you would never have written this story yourself."

Now, without Emma, Diana pulled into the driveway, but she stopped short of the garage. Paul's bicycle wasn't propped up against the side of it, but this wasn't one of his teaching days, so Diana supposed he had gone to his office or to the library to do research. Maybe he was already planning his Alfred M. Fuller lecture for the fall.

Diana opened the back door, which was unlocked, and stepped into the kitchen, kicking her shoes off as she went.

The house was quiet.

The breakfast things, as always, were unmoved.

Outside, in the sky, a bit of yellow sun cracked through the purple clouds, and a bruise-colored light shone through the screen door. Diana turned on the radio over the refrigerator and began to tidy up.

Dr. Laura was talking to what sounded like a very young man.

"It's not fair, I don't think," he said.

"What's fair?" the talk show host asked.

He didn't answer.

"She told me she was using birth control," he said.

"Well," Dr. Laura said, "did you ever ask her what she'd want to do if the birth control *failed*?"

"No," he said.

"You should have," Dr. Laura said.

"I'm too young to have a baby," he said.

"That may well be," Dr. Laura said, "but you're having one now, so you'd better grow up."

It sounded as though the boy were beginning to cry.

Diana stopped and listened, holding a dish towel in her hand.

The radio crying became louder and louder, then turned into what sounded like a howl—a newborn baby, or an animal in pain—and Diana dropped the dish towel and reached quickly for the dial on the radio, spinning it away from that station. But still, in the static, she could hear the howl, and something else....

Laughter?

A man's deep laughter?

Then it was replaced by silence, the sound of electricity and stars.

It's quiet here.

No one is in the church behind them, and no cars pass by on the road. A few blackbirds scream from the trees, but they don't seem angry. They're just making noise to cut holes in the silence.

The gravestones are aged and weathered, and the names on most of them have been washed away by time and rain.

The grass, a lush lime green, whispers as they walk on it.

Toward the back of the cemetery, the markers grow smaller, closer to the ground, and the girls bend down to read what's been chiseled beneath a little angel whose face is tilted upward and whose features have turned to soap through a century of weeping:

Close your eyes and weep no more, Little John has gone before.

Beside Little John's angel is a lamb guarding the grave of Little John's brother:

Beloved infant of Sarah and Vaughn.

The two boys were born years apart but died on the same day. April 29, 1888.

The girls read the names and dates on the graves around them in silence, wandering.

"They're all kids," one of them finally says.

"Jesus," the other one says.

WHEN ALL OF THE BREAKFAST DISHES WERE PUT AWAY, Diana headed upstairs.

The yellow sun had been extinguished briefly by a swift cloud passing, and when Diana stepped into the bedroom, it was completely dark. She switched on the overhead light.

At first she didn't gasp. *One, two, three, four* seconds passed before she realized what she was seeing, and then she inhaled sharp and fast and put her hand to her mouth. She leaped backward, and Timmy jumped from the bed, ran past her in a bolt of blackness, then down the stairs.

Timmy.

She was able in the split second before he was out of sight to see him clearly, and she *knew* it was Timmy.

Not the Timmy of the last two years of his life, but the Timmy of her own youth. Fat and glossy and black.

For a moment Diana couldn't move. She felt as if she'd been punched in the stomach—low, just above her womb—and the dull shock of it was absorbed by her whole body. It traveled in both directions along her spine....

And then the pain lodged itself in her head, which she held in both hands, closing her eyes tightly before she opened them again to the quiet orderliness of the bedroom she shared with her husband.

Roses on the wallpaper.

White curtains on the windows.

She sat down on the hope chest she'd been given by her mother when Diana announced her engagement to Paul—the one her mother had filled with bedsheets and dish towels in the months before they were married.

It was solidly built of wood, and now she kept sweaters in it. Sweaters and nighties...

Then she realized, of course, that it was some kind of mistake.

Some cat, some neighborhood cat, had gotten into their house.

Maybe Paul had left the back door open when he took out the garbage that morning.

And then she started to laugh—harder than she'd expected

to laugh. She laughed until the tears fell onto her pink cashmere tank top.

Timmy had been buried in the yard.

Timmy was dead, was ashes.

By now, less than ashes.

And then there was the quick stab of it, the memory of Timmy collapsing slowly in her arms after the veterinarian administered the shot. The way Timmy had relaxed into himself in the most terrible, total way imaginable, in a way that didn't make Diana feel in the least that death would come as a comfort, come as a sleep, but that it would, instead, be a complete annihilation of everything—the self, the soul, the world...

Remembering Timmy like that made Diana swallow the laughter and tears and put her hand, again, to her head, where the ache had returned, completely concentrated now at her right temple, an entirely cold and brilliant pain.

But whose cat was that, and where had it gone?

Diana started down the stairs.

She had to hold tightly to the railing because the sun had not yet emerged from the cloud and the stairwell was utterly dark, as dark as night.

"Here, kitty-kitty-kitty," she called, as she had always called to Timmy, but in a weak and wavering voice.

Suddenly rain began to pound on the roof. A hard, full rain. And when she got downstairs, Diana couldn't see. She turned on all the lamps as she went, looking around—under the couch, behind the chair.

Timmy—or the cat who resembled Timmy, the one who had gotten into their house somehow—wasn't there.

Again she called.

But Timmy had never come when he was called.

Timmy was the only cat she'd ever had. Maybe all cats were that way.

Diana went into the kitchen. By now she was rubbing her eyes. Could she simply have imagined it? Could she have seen a cat that wasn't there? Was there some cluster of cells in her brain that had *Timmy* imprinted on them? Had they fired randomly at some sensory trigger? Perhaps the smell of rain about to fall?

She turned the light on in the kitchen, and he yowled.

Timmy. He was standing in the kitchen by the refrigerator in the place where they'd kept his dried food and water. He nudged the edge of the refrigerator as he'd always done, rubbing his face against it affectionately, then he looked casually up at Diana.

"Timmy?"

She reached down and scratched behind his ears.

Timmy purred, dry and loud.

Light and Shadow

"Diana," Paul said over the telephone when she reached him in his office.

Timmy was curled up on her lap, fast asleep.

She'd opened a can of tuna fish for him, and he'd wolfed it, licked the bowl until even the aftertaste of tuna would have been long gone.

Diana held the phone to her ear with one hand, and with the other she petted the cat.

"Diana," he repeated, "black cats do tend to resemble one another, you know."

"I know," Diana said. She knew it had sounded defensive, so she laughed. "It's just strange, the resemblance. And how did he get in?"

"Are you sure it's a *he*?"

"Yeah," she told him, "I checked."

"He could have gotten in a million different ways. Most likely one of us left the door open this morning. Or we might have some gap between the basement and the front porch. Something we never noticed. Maybe he got in through the attic."

"I know," Diana said.

And it was true.

She *did* know.

There had to have been a million gaps in the foundation of a house this old, holes in the roof, places where something could sneak in and out without being seen. And the cat—the cat, though it bore such a resemblance to Timmy—the cat was *not* Timmy. No one needed to tell her that. Timmy...

Diana had watched for years with her own eyes as Timmy had aged and decayed. She'd been right there with the veterinarian when the injection was given. She'd been holding Timmy. This cat in her lap was not that cat.

"Are you keeping it?" Paul asked.

The question sounded strange to her. Are *you* keeping the cat. Surely he meant *we*....

"If no one comes looking for him, if no one puts an ad in the paper, I don't see why—"

"That's fine," Paul said. "I was just asking."

"It'll be nice for Emma."

Paul said nothing.

"When will you be home?" Diana asked.

He told her he'd be home early. He was having trouble working. He'd see her that afternoon.

Driving back into Briar Hill, they stop at a roadside fruit stand.

An old man and his old wife are selling California peaches.

The old man has skin like leather, but the old woman is draped in a brown shawl, and she wears a man's fishing cap low on her face. What they can see of her skin looks perfectly smooth. The skin of someone who has avoided the sun all of her life.

The old man doesn't look at the girls. He simply takes the money they offer him for the peaches, and points at the bushel baskets and says, "Take your fruit."

The old woman watches them from under the brim of the khaki fishing cap.

One of the girls can feel the old woman's eyes on the rose tattoo on her hip.

A pickup pulls up at the corner, turning left onto the country road, and two boys inside it whistle and shout out the window.

"Baby! Hey!"

They could be shouting at either one of the girls, but the one with the rose tattoo on her hip cannot look up from the bushel basket of peaches. She feels something warm, like tears or blood, smooth itself out from her throat to her hips.

The boys, whistling.

The old man and woman scowling.

The bushels of fruit in the sun—ripe.

A small cloud of fruit flies hovering almost invisibly over the fruit.

The sun like a burning Earth overhead.

But why would she dress this way—the shorts, the tattoo, the spaghetti straps, the gold ring in her belly button—if she didn't want to be looked at?

The girls eat the peaches in the car.

The taste is blindingly sweet, but the juice runs all over so that everything the girls touch until they wash their hands will turn to sweetness and stick to the tips of their fingers.

AFTER A WHILE TIMMY JUMPED OFF HER LAP.

He leaped up onto the couch then and curled to sleep in his favorite spot—a place where the floral pattern had been worn away from years of sleep and restless kneading.

Timmy was an outdoor cat, so he'd had his claws. Every piece of furniture in their house, and every rug, still bore Timmy's marks.

Diana stood up from the chair. She was feeling good again. Something had been returned to her... changed, but hers. He was purring and snoring when she left the living room to go to her studio, and she closed the kitchen door behind her when she left the house.

Outside, the rain had stopped, but there was still the distant rumbling of thunder, sporadic flashes of lightning near the horizon. The air smelled like tin. It was steamy. There were worms lying bloated on the driveway.

Inside the garage it was dark, but once Diana had climbed the stairs and opened the door to her studio, she turned on the light, and she saw the sketch of the two teenagers, the one she'd drawn the day before, still on her drawing board.

It was one of her favorite moments, the one in which she approached a drawing she'd recently done but which she hadn't looked at closely yet, hadn't really *seen*. She'd been away from it for a day, so looking at it now was like looking at a stranger's piece, or like something one of her students had drawn. It was the only time when she could be critical and admiring of her own work.

And this work was pretty good.

There was a sense of composition in it. Neither too centered nor too symmetrical, but not lacking those qualities, either.

The boy and the girl were near the right corner of the drawing, almost as if the artist were seeing them out of the corner of her eye. The informality of the girl's arm flung across her eyes was perfect. Unposed. Real. And her cigarette in the other hand was the right, unsentimental touch. The girl was beautiful, and so was the boy. His arms were thin. The girl's breasts lay flat against her chest as most girls' breasts lie, in this position, no matter how young and firm their bodies are.

And the light was right.

It glinted off the surface of the pool, rippling but jagged, like measured brain waves.

And the shadows cast by the edge of the Ellsworths' garage were creeping slowly from the teenagers' legs to their torsos, which made the brightness of the sun on their limbs and faces appear even brighter.

Diana was pleased.

Then there was a flash of lightning followed by a crack of thunder so loud and close that she gasped. The light in her studio surged and flickered once, and then it went out.

"Shit," Diana said, louder and more angrily than she'd meant to, and then the headache began again.

She'd forgotten about the headache...

Had it ever gone away, or had she simply, for a while, not registered the pain?

Another flash of lightning, and in the half second of it,

Diana saw nothing but her own drawing, which seemed altered in the brevity and brilliance.

The image.

The darkness.

Another flash. Again the image. The cigarette, Diana realized.

Darkness.

Another millisecond of brilliance.

The cigarette.

She hadn't drawn it.

This girl didn't smoke.

Diana rubbed her eyes and started to feel her way backward. She bumped the chair too hard with her foot, and it crashed, and again Diana said, "Shit." Her heart was racing. The darkness became total, and the rain on the roof was deafening. Between the darkness and the muffled drumming of the rain, Diana felt panicked to return to the world of her senses. She couldn't hear. She couldn't see. She felt silly for feeling frightened. It was just a thunderstorm. It was just an image she'd remembered differently than she'd actually drawn it. She was a grown woman. Safe neighborhood. Good life...

And then another flash of lightning broke into the blackness, and again it was her drawing she saw—the white window of it, and the teenage girl, who'd moved her arm away from her face and was looking back at Diana.

Glass

By the time she got back into the house, the lights had come back on. The clock on the microwave was blinking, and the refrigerator was purring loudly, as it always did after a surge.

Diana went to it and put her head against it. There was something comforting about the machine noise of it, the soft hum of its motor. It struck her as mysterious, suddenly, the solid reliability of it, the way a machine, without food or encouragement, does one job well until it dies.

The pain seemed to pass from her head into the refrigerator, though she knew it would come back when she was no longer resting against the solid hum.

Tylenol. Motrin. She needed...

Diana wasn't surprised to feel the cat rubbing up against her bare legs, but still she inhaled.

His nose was cold on her ankles, a familiar sensation. He looked up at her and opened his mouth to reveal his white teeth and hot-pink tongue. He made a noise that was halfway between a cry and a purr . . . a growl?

Timmy.

Diana moved away from the refrigerator, expecting the headache to return to her suddenly and completely, but it didn't. She exhaled. She opened the refrigerator and took out a carton of low-fat milk and poured some of it into the emptied bowl. There wasn't much in the house to feed a cat. She'd have to go to the store for cat food and litter and a litter box, since surely they'd thrown Timmy's things out long ago.

He lapped happily at the milk.

They have fathers.

One lives alone in an apartment across town. He works at Circuit City selling entertainment systems during the day, and at night he plays saxophone in a jazz quartet. He looks younger than he is. He has an earring. His name is Robert. It's hard to remember to call him Dad. Everyone else calls him Bop.

The other girl's father moved long ago to a nearby town. He has a son and a wife and a computer software company.

Their mothers speak of their fathers with too much intimacy. It's terrible to think that their mothers and fathers were once in love with each other. It means that love is nothing but bitterness, wistfulness, oblivion—although still, for some reason, the girls believe in it. They imagine their own happy marriages vividly, as if they'd been born with an image of it imprinted on their dreams, the way birds are born knowing how to make their species' nests without ever having to be taught.

They think about their fathers on the second Saturday of every month, on Christmas Eve, their birthdays, and on Father's Day.

Father's Day.

It rises out of June like smoke, smelling of barbecue sauce.

Bermuda shorts, beer cans, and the sound of a lawn mower starting up—that gasping roar, over and over, like a wild animal being trained. *Baseball games on the radio, a hushed and imaginary diamond far away. In the aluminum toolshed, the garden hose coiled up like a huge snake, waiting.* They are the Hallmark images that are attached to the idea of fatherhood but not to their own fathers.

Next Sunday is Father's Day.

The girls go together to a store downtown called Precious Moments, where they buy matching glass beer mugs and have *Happy Father's Day* engraved on them in a kind of stiff, feminine cursive written by a machine with a very sharp needle at its tip.

The clerk who sells them the mugs shrouds them in tissue paper and bubble wrap so they won't break.

DIANA FELT TIRED.

She lay down upstairs on the bed and tried closing her eyes, but she felt too nervous to nap. What was it? She wondered without knowing what she was wondering about.

Something was happening.

Had it just begun in the last few days?

She was too young for menopause. But something, she felt, was changing. It had to do with her body as well as her mind.

Was this what happened with middle age?

An accumulation of experiences and things tumbling toward you?

Did the past start to bleed into the present, as if the past were red towels washed in warm water with white sheets?

Haunted.

Her body. Her mind. Her neighborhood. Her town.

She'd inhabited these things for a long time now.

She'd done things she regretted.

She saw the life she'd lived, the accumulation of its details, like a huge wheel rolling toward her, rolling down a hill.

She liked to think of herself as the kind of woman who saw the cup as *half full.* She tried to look on the bright side. She had long practiced the art of avoiding morbid thoughts. She rarely read the newspaper. When an accident or murder was reported on the evening news, Diana turned the television off. Paul liked to kid her that her presence at any gathering "cleansed" the atmosphere, that in her presence no one told dirty jokes or relayed disturbing anecdotes.

She hoped he was right.

She knew the kind of woman she could have been—ironic, a little angry, a bit too loud. Diana saw those women coming, and when they opened their mouths with some half-decent bit of gossip or some shocking crime report they wanted to talk about as if it were funny, Diana simply looked at them, let them talk, but didn't approve of them, and they knew it.

Even her drawings were simple revelations of goodness. It was probably why she hadn't gone on to greater success. It was an age in which the shocking image was celebrated, but Diana wasn't interested in making that kind of art.

She didn't even experiment with line and form. To her those

elements were pure. There was nothing sinister about what she drew. The shadows were still shadows and the light was light.

However, for a while, she'd been someone else. Vaguely she knew it, but only in the way that one knows that nine months were spent in a womb once. There was the evidence to prove it, but the experience itself was as lost as if it had never been.

She couldn't have been the only one who felt this way.

The time period in which she'd been a teenager had led to indulgences and excesses no other generation had ever known, and now millions of those teenage girls were soccer moms. Diana had *seen* those soccer moms when they were teenagers—when they'd been promiscuous, tattooed, pierced in intimate places. She couldn't be the only one who'd grown up and become a mother and found herself to be a complete stranger to the girl she'd been—but haunted. Definitely haunted. That girl she'd been *was* her now, although the woman she'd become wouldn't have trusted that girl with her wedding china, with her car keys, let alone her home, her child, her *life*.

Diana opened her eyes.

No sense lying there.

Every woman had a past.

She got out of bed.

She'd dust. She'd straighten Paul's study. It would surprise him when he got home. Maybe she'd go to the store before she got Emma, and she'd pick out a nice little gift for Paul, something to celebrate his lecture.

She turned the light on in his study, and as it always did, the smell of it—musty books and Paul—and the sight of his shelves, the chaos of papers on his desk and on the floor, reminded her of her love for him. That love, the feeling of it, began at her lips and smoothed warmly down her throat and filled her chest.

It had always been like that.

She'd start with the garbage can, she decided. It was overflowing with ripped and wadded-up sheets of yellow legal paper next to his desk, but before she took the can out of his study to empty it, she sat in his desk chair and looked around. She ran her hand over the pine drawer in which he kept his pens, his calculator, his rolls of tape and boxes of staples.

She opened the drawer and looked in.

It wasn't exactly in order, but there were his things. A tape measure, too. A pair of scissors.

She closed the door and pulled the chair in to his desk, which was piled high with books. Most of them were tattered, ancient. Some were in Italian. Some in Medieval English. At least three of them were in Latin. One must have been Greek.

She pushed a book away from the notepad on Paul's desk and looked down at his familiar, beloved handwriting . . . loopy and jagged at the same time. He always wrote in black ink.

. . . *Conscience is the voice of God in the nature and heart of man* . . .

Next to it, he'd written the date at the top of the page, and because it was yesterday's, Diana imagined that this was the beginning of notes for his lecture.

It gave her an idea for a gift.

There was a place where they etched names and inscriptions on glass plates or mugs or ashtrays. Precious Moments. She'd had a wine glass engraved for him years before, for his fiftieth birthday: *For the man I will always love, on his 50th birthday.*

She'd have a matching one engraved with these words to celebrate his lecture.

She tore the piece of paper from the pad.

Glare

The sun had come out. There were puddles of glare in the garden where the light bounced off the gathered rain, and steam rose from them. It would be a warm and humid afternoon if it stayed clear. One of the first really summery days of the season. Laundromat weather, Paul called it.

The rain had beaten the daisies down, and they looked weak. Diana couldn't remember why she'd disliked them so much. Perhaps there were just too many of them now that they'd begun to spread. She'd separate them, dig some up, transplant them to the sunny side of the garage, where the tulips had already lived and died for the year. She could work around the bulbs. Next spring one brilliant batch of flowers would follow the other. Diana was no gardener, but she'd been watching flowers bloom and die long enough to have some idea of how she might time them to keep something blooming in any given spot from May to September, if the spot got sun.

Maybe it hadn't been the daisies that had bothered her. It was just their crowded conditions. Still, slumped from the rain, they already seemed to be stirring, turning their faces toward her, or toward the sun.

She looked away from them and noticed her neighbor Rita Smith.

Diana waved, and Rita Smith waved back from over in her own yard, where she was hacking away with a pair of long shears at a forsythia bush. It was something Rita did every year after the yellow blossoms faded. Branches and leaves were littered all over Rita's front yard.

Neither woman smiled at the other. For years they hadn't spoken more than a couple of words to one another . . . since the afternoon Timmy had found and massacred a nest of baby rabbits in Rita's backyard.

Timmy, Diana had tried to explain, was just doing what cats do.

Timmy, said Rita—who was not much older than Diana, but childless, husbandless, and at least fifty pounds overweight—ought to be kept indoors, where he couldn't kill helpless and innocent things.

Keeping Timmy indoors was out of the question, Diana had tried to explain. Timmy was an outdoor cat. And he was old. There was no way such a change in Timmy's lifestyle could be achieved. . . .

Rita had ended the conversation abruptly by saying, "Please keep your cat off my property," her jowly face turning pink.

Diana had lifted a shoulder and shook her head, trying to indicate that it was impossible. *How* could she keep Timmy out of Rita Smith's yard? He couldn't be put on a leash. She couldn't spend every minute of the day monitoring his whereabouts.

But in the end, it didn't matter. Not much later, as if Rita were some kind of witch, Timmy had begun to age rapidly. His outdoor adventures were limited to lying in the daisies, breathing shallowly.

And then he died.

But her neighbor held a permanent grudge against Diana.

And now Timmy was back. Diana bit her lip. She couldn't help smiling to herself. She thought that she'd noticed Rita Smith glance disapprovingly at the short denim skirt she was still wearing, or maybe she was looking disapprovingly at Diana's long and slender legs, smooth in the sunlight.

Fuck you, Diana thought.

They drive to the mall.

It's the middle of the afternoon, a weekday, and the mall is nearly empty. Outside, the sun is magnificent in the sky—high and fiery and pouring golden light all over the tarry summer streets and the cars, which send up sharp edges and arrows of light as they pass under that sun and the perfectly blue sky it's burning in.

Inside the mall it's a parody of a summer day. The sound of water splashing against rocks. The breathy music of flutes floating on the air-conditioned air. A fluorescent whiteness cleansing everything as if in preparation for surgery, or burial, or birth—a chemical, medical whiteness.

In the basement of Briar Hill High, there is a recycle room, and the students have to take turns lugging bins and bundles of recyclable waste there each week. Both girls have taken their turns in that room, which is cold but also sweaty and full of moths—fat brown ones that don't move. They look mummified, or freeze-dried, wings folded up on top of the cardboard boxes and stacks of gray newspaper. It's impossible to tell if those moths are dead or alive, or something else—lost in some sort of deep moth sleep.

And what would they be dreaming?

The mall, empty, on a day this bright and sunny might be a dead moth's dream.

The girls are wearing shorts and skimpy tops and sandals, and they feel coldly naked in the mall when they first enter it. Conspicuously out of place. The heels of their sandals sound hard and loud on the linoleum. The mall is so empty, it's hard to know where to walk. They keep veering away from one another accidentally, then back again.

The mall is full of things they already own—cheap, bright things. Tube tops, tennis shoes, denim skirts, jeans.

Stuffed animals, board games, CDs, perfume, lipstick, cubic zirconia earrings.

The salespeople are bored. They want to be outside, in the real sun, the actual world. They stand around and watch the girls passing through the merchandise, fingering a few things, laughing, and they don't offer to help.

"Let's get out of here," one of the girls says to the other.

The other laughs and turns around, walking fast in the direction from which they've come.

They run awkwardly on the slippery linoleum until they reach the glass doors to the parking lot, then hurry back out into the world.

"That was creepy," one of the girls says, starting the car.

The other turns on the radio and says, "God, it's good to be *alive* again."

They laugh, and drive off.

THE AREA OF RESTAURANTS, BOOKSTORES, CLOTHING boutiques, and coffee shops near campus was nearly empty.

Class had been over for a month, and most of the students had gone to wherever it was they went between semesters. Only the summer school students, and the ones who worked or played in the area, had stayed behind. It was the time of year that Diana liked Briar Hill best. A kind of limbo. Beautiful weather, flowers in bloom, but no one there to clutter it up. And she liked the kinds of students who stayed behind. They looked relaxed. The girls wore long skirts. The boys wore cutoffs. They had stringy hair and smoked clove cigarettes. On the commons lawn at that moment, two such stringy-haired boys were throwing a Frisbee. Their naked torsos glistened in the sun. Though those boys were old enough to go to war, they were playing a child's game with total concentration under a sun the color of margarine that afternoon. They ran and leaped, chasing the bright piece of plastic that sailed between them on the breeze.

The absurdity of it made Diana smile.

She found a parking spot easily, which was another benefit of summer in Briar Hill, and she fed a few coins to the parking meter, then crossed the street to the Precious Moments store, where she would have the wine glass engraved for Paul.

She had her page of notebook paper folded in her purse.

. . . *Conscience is the voice of God in the nature and heart of man* . . .

There was a smell in the air that reminded her of semen. Some kind of tree, she supposed. The leaves on that tree. She'd smelled it a million times before and had often wondered if she was the only person in the world who'd made such an association. To her the connection seemed obvious. In the summer the leaves of that tree—she looked around her but couldn't tell which tree it would have been—shed something clean and physical smelling into the breeze. No one could argue that the flowers smelled like sex, *were* like sex...cupped, honeyed, opening themselves to the world...

But she'd never heard anyone mention the obvious, permeating aroma of sperm that was released by the trees.

Diana exhaled in disappointment when she saw the out-of-business sign in the store window.

Since when?

She went to the door, anyway, and tried to open it, but it was, of course, locked.

She read the sign again.

OUT OF BUSINESS

Then she put her face to the glass door and peered in.

It was dark inside, though Diana could see that it was still full of glass gifts. Apparently it hadn't been out of business long enough to sell off the inventory.

She went over to the window at the front of the store, put her hands around her face to block the sun, and looked.

The store seemed to be empty of people, but the glass inside appeared dustless. So many clear and fragile things. The light from the sun behind her caused her own shadow to fall inside the store and stretch from the window to a shelf full of exactly the kind of wine glass she'd wanted to have engraved for Paul.

The wine glasses shone brightly, as if to taunt her.

Everything in that darkness did.

It was like looking at the complicated inner workings of a Swiss watch.

Crystals and brilliance.

Or the inside of a television. A computer. An ice cave. A pure heart. A vacant mind. Heaven . . .

Or a hospital laboratory. Hundreds and hundreds of tubes and vials, clean and scrubbed on the shelves.

Then her shadow moved inside the store. It crossed the wooden floors and reached its hand up and took down one of the wine glasses from the shelf, then turned toward Diana with the glass in its hand.

Diana began to breathe faster, but she pressed her face closer to the window until she could see what it was:

Not a shadow, but a young woman. Her face stepped out of Diana's shadow into the light, and she, too, looked startled when she saw Diana.

The young woman was blond and long-legged and looked enough like Diana to have *been* her if not for the space of two decades between them. Like Diana, she was wearing a short denim skirt. But she was also wearing a cropped T-shirt, and her midriff was bare. There was a ring in her belly button, and another just above her eyebrow.

When she saw Diana, the young woman hurried from the shelf to the glass door and unlocked it. There was the sound of bells when the door opened.

"Ma'am? Can I help you?"

The young woman was much more beautiful than Diana had realized before she saw her closely. Her skin was flawless in the bright light, and so pale that a cool blue vein could be seen at her temple. Her hair was the kind of flat, flaxen blond that looked like a sheet of water in the sun.

"I was just surprised to see the store was out of business," Diana said. "I was hoping to have something engraved. One of those." Diana nodded at the wine glass in the girl's hand.

"I'm sorry," she said. "We just closed, like two days ago. They hired me to, like, inventory and clean up."

"Oh," Diana said. "No chance I could maybe just buy one of those?..." She nodded again at the wine glass in the young woman's hand. "It matches one I bought for my husband some years ago. Maybe I could have it engraved somewhere else."

The girl looked at the wine glass and then at Diana. "Here," she said, handing it to Diana, "you can have it."

"Oh, I—" Diana hesitated but she reached out to take the glass, afraid that the girl would let go of it, that it would smash between them on the concrete.

"It's just a wine glass," the young woman said, as if Diana had mistaken it for something else.

The girl's teeth were like a string of pearls, so perfect when she smiled. The teeth of someone who'd never sipped coffee or eaten cherry pie. Then she closed the door and locked it.

Diana carried the wine glass carefully back to the minivan. It seemed so weightless and fragile in her hand, much more so than the one she'd had engraved years before. Maybe it wasn't a match. This glass felt like air, like nothing, in her hand.

It didn't matter. She'd have it engraved. It was the thought that counted.

Diana unlocked the passenger's side door to the minivan and placed the wine glass carefully down on the backseat. She had nothing—no tissue paper, no bubble wrap—to protect it with, but she thought she'd just leave it there for now, go to the bookstore and buy a newspaper, read the newspaper at the coffee shop, then come back and wrap the glass in the paper before she drove off to pick up Emma.

She was just locking the minivan again, opening her purse to fish out a few more coins for the meter, when she saw him out of the corner of her eye.

Paul.

It wasn't a coincidence, of course. His office was only a block over from here in a huge white-pillared building called Angel Hall.

He was walking in the opposite direction of that building and didn't see Diana. He was on the opposite side of the street. He was talking as he strode along the sidewalk... moving his hands as he did when he was explaining something or was excited. It was one of the first things Diana had been attracted to... one of the first things she'd noticed about him from the fourth row of the classroom where she sat watching and listening.

Diana didn't bother with the coins. She looked both ways to make sure no cars were coming, although she was on a one-way street. Then she began to hurry across. She didn't call his name; she wanted to surprise him. She ran toward him across the black river of tar between one curb and the next.

On the other side her husband was walking down the sidewalk with a girl.

The girl had short blond hair, cut close to the scalp, and she was wearing a wraparound skirt that reached to about two inches above her knees. It was an exotic Indian pattern of flowers and spiky leaves, henna red with gold thread sewn through the flower petals. As the breeze lifted and parted it, even Diana, from the middle of the road, could see one bare thigh. And a tight black tank top. The girl had large, loose breasts. Her hair was so light and short it glittered, and Diana's husband was smiling, gesturing, looking straight ahead, while the girl with the glittering hair watched the side of his face.

With one hand the girl played self-consciously with an earring—a long beaded and silver thing. Her other hand was tucked casually into the back pocket of Paul's jeans.

First, Diana felt the breeze of it.

Then she saw a glint of sun on chrome.

But she ignored it, and kept walking.

The minivan was traveling the wrong way down the one-way street, and it was speeding, which was why Diana never saw it. She heard it first—the squealing of the brakes, the blast of the horn—and smelled burning rubber before she felt it... something bright exploding against her temple. It sent her flying in the direction from which she'd come. She saw her purse in the air and watched the slow explosion of it—coins and credit cards and blood—land at the curb near her husband's feet.

Part Four

Birds

When she opened her eyes again, Diana was looking into Paul's.

Behind him an overweight woman who'd been weeping was holding her own upper arms, rocking back and forth. Both the overweight woman and Paul were on their knees.

"Where is she?" Diana asked.

"Who?" Paul asked. "Diana. Are you okay? Are you hurt?"

Diana felt the side of her face, the place where she'd felt the brightness enter her. She expected to feel blood or pain, but there was nothing.

"Can you sit up?"

Diana sat up and looked around.

The minivan that had grazed her looked exactly like her own except that the rearview mirror on the passenger's side had been shattered, and on the bumper there was a sticker that said CHOOSE LIFE.

The overweight woman had a purse that looked like Diana's in her lap.

"Oh, thank god you're all right," the woman said.

A small group of students was standing on the side of the street Diana had been trying to reach.

There were about six of them. They were thin and wore dark makeup around their eyes. *Goths.* Diana remembered Goths. In the hierarchy of students at Briar Hill High, Goths had been the lowest, but Diana had always felt an affection for them... the way they pretended not to hear the insults hurled at them by Jocks and Preps in the hallways, the way they stuck together like a flock of crows in the cafeteria.

Whether these students were boys or girls, Diana couldn't tell. They were all thin and wore black jeans, black T-shirts. "Who are they?" she whispered to Paul, but he didn't turn to look. He just helped Diana to her feet, brushed off the back of her denim skirt. The overweight woman stood up, too. She handed Diana her purse.

Diana looked at it.

It was a tan suede thing with a silver clasp.

Diana could have sworn she'd seen blood explode from it when the purse hit the curb, but now there was no blood.

"I gathered up your cards," the woman said. "I think everything's in there."

Paul was holding on to Diana's arm, but she pulled away from him.

She wanted to talk to the students on the other side of the street, the ones who had been waiting for her—to ask them what had happened, what had they seen?—but when she looked again, they were already gone.

"Let go of me," she said to Paul sharply.

"Diana," he said, "you need to sit down. Come on. You've had a shock."

"I said let go of me," she said.

The overweight woman looked from Diana to Paul. She had dry red hair but perfectly smooth skin and very green eyes. She radiated bumbling kindness, like a comical goddess. Her cheeks were still wet with her tears. She said to Paul, "Should we call an ambulance?"

Paul shook his head.

"I'm not afraid of being ticketed," the woman said, and she began to weep again. "This is my fault. I deserve to be in jail."

"No," Paul said, not looking at the woman. "She was just grazed. It was just the shock."

Diana looked at the woman, then at Paul, and said, "I just want to get out of here."

"Here," Paul said, taking her arm again.

"I *said* let *go* of me,"

He did, and she turned to walk away from him. He called her name to her back, but she ignored him. The keys to her minivan were inside her purse. She fished them out. When she'd unlocked the driver's side, she got in and turned the keys in the ignition, backed up carefully, pulled out of her parking space, and drove away. In the rearview mirror she could see Paul and the overweight woman still standing in the street, which had remained somehow emptied of traffic. They watched her go.

Diana trembled as she drove, and her vision was blurred. It seemed to her that the parked cars, the pedestrians, the storefronts and speed limit signs were being passed at an incredible speed, but when she looked at the speedometer, she saw that she was driving only twenty-five miles an hour. When a woman pushing a stroller stepped off the curb, Diana swerved, honked, and missed hitting the baby in the stroller by what seemed to her to be only inches—though she could see the mother's face clearly as she passed, and the mother looked calm, curious, but unconcerned—and the lurching as she swerved sent the wine glass Diana had left in the backseat flying onto the floor of the minivan.

She glanced behind her.

The stem had cracked neatly away from the bowl.

When she looked in the rearview mirror again, Diana could see the mother watching her drive away. That mother was younger than Diana and closer than she appeared, fading and miniaturized in the mirror.

They take turns sleeping over at each other's mothers' apartments.

One girl sleeps on the inflatable mattress on the floor at the foot of the other girl's twin bed. Mostly they lie awake in their places in the darkness and talk. Sometimes they start to laugh so hard they have to put pillows over their faces so they won't wake one of their mothers, asleep in the next room...

She has to go to work in the morning.

They laugh about Nate. The day they saw him outside the CD shop. How they'd been too nervous and awed to stop, to say a word to him.

"In the fall," one of the girls says—the one who is still a virgin—"in the fall I'm just going to walk straight up to him and say, 'How about going for a drive with me, Nate?'"

"Go, girl," the other says. But it makes her nervous, this innocence in her friend. There's more to it, she wants to tell her. There's . . .

They laugh about Mr. McCleod. The teenage skeleton he's in love with. They laugh about Sandy Ellsworth, who came to school so stoned one afternoon that during gym she started up a conversation with a punching bag.

"No way!" says the one who wasn't there.

"I swear to god. She bumped into the punching bag, and she turned around, and she was, like, 'Watch where you're going, asshole. I was here first,' but then she started to mellow out and she was, like, 'Do you know what we're supposed to be doing right now?' and she just stood there like the punching bag was going to answer."

"Wow," the other one says. From where she lies on the floor, the ceiling of her friend's bedroom is glossy with darkness, and far away. She can hear her friend's poodle, Muppet, snoring quietly on the twin bed above her. "Wow. That girl is going to have a serious brain cell shortage when she's middle-aged."

"*If* she lives that long."

The subject of Sandy Ellsworth's future makes them think about their own.

They try out different ones—colleges, husbands, children, careers.

The names of the children change from one future to the next.

Tricia, Allison, Emma, Irene . . . girls.

Jeffrey, Kyle, Cody, Logan . . . boys.

But none of the names ever seems quite right.

Nor do the futures. Though there is one out there waiting for each of them, two futures tucked away somewhere with their names on them—futures which, when they come, will seem right, will seem like the inevitable futures, the ones everything they'd ever thought and done had led them to blindly—right now they can't begin to imagine them.

DIANA PULLED UP IN FRONT OF OUR LADY OF FATIMA just as the school bell rang.

The orange double doors burst open, and a chaos of windbreakers and pumping legs flew out. In the colorful fragments, Diana couldn't see her daughter, but it was often that way. She'd stare at the pieces of this scene on the hill outside her daughter's elementary school until Emma's image emerged from it, sharp-angled and perfectly clear, running toward the waiting minivan.

Diana watched.

Here and there she could make out the face of a little girl she recognized. A girl with terrible red hair and skin so pale she looked as if she'd been dug up. A blond girl with glasses, a girl who'd once come to the house to play with Emma before she'd narrowed her friends down to only Sarah Ann Salerno and Mary Olivet, who were both dark.

The blond girl, Diana seemed to remember, couldn't eat ice cream because she was allergic to milk products. Diana had run out to the store to buy Popsicles...

Now that blond girl stumbled and fell on the concrete steps that led down the hill, away from the school.

Diana inhaled sharply. The girl had only fallen down one step, and she appeared to be unhurt, but it could have been worse. Those stairs, Diana realized, had no railing. They were dangerous. Something ought to be done . . . a strict rule that the girls could not run down those stairs after school. She would speak to Sister Beatrice about it right away.

When the little blond girl tried to stand back up, another girl, running past her, knocked her back down, and the blond girl's backpack slipped down her arm, and a book and some pencils spilled out.

When the little blond sat up to try to retrieve one of the books, another girl bumped into her, and she fell forward again, and suddenly there were even more girls pouring out from between the double doors, chattering and skipping and running down the concrete steps, oblivious to the one who'd fallen. She'd never seen so many girls exit the school at the end of the day. Where had they come from? The little girl who'd fallen would be trampled.

Diana got out of the minivan and started to hurry toward her. Was she imagining it, or did the child have blood on the side of her face now?

She ran into the sea of little girls, against the tide of little girls galloping and screaming down the concrete steps, oblivious. She tried to be gentle as she pushed them out of her way, hurrying toward the blond girl who had by now been knocked to her side, who wasn't moving at all.

There *was* blood on her face.

She was only a few feet from the girl when an older, taller girl smacked directly into Diana, and it knocked the wind out of her. She put her hand to her chest and had to stop running, had to stand, without breathing, on the steps as the girls parted around her, not even glancing at her.

Diana swallowed, trying not to panic. She knew that the

breath would come back. This had happened before. Once, she'd been running on the playground, chasing another girl, and she'd tripped and fallen down flat in the grass . . .

It had seemed to her then, lying in the emerald grass unable to breathe, that she lived a whole lifetime waiting for her breath to come back. That time, she hadn't known that it ever *would* come back. A small group of children had gathered around her, and their faces were pale and featureless and inconsequential above her. There was nothing they could do, Diana realized. They, like her, were made of nothing more material than clouds. If she couldn't catch her breath again, they would simply disappear. . . .

Diana looked up at the sky now, as she had then, and it was full of glitter.

It was as if it were snowing in the middle of June.

Or was she looking so closely now, in this moment between one breath and the next, that she could see the atoms, see the molecules out of which everything had been made?

Then the glitter seemed to shake itself out like a sheet in the breeze, and Diana's breath came back to her in one cool stab that entered her like light and was scented with yeast, curry, cloves . . . *life.* When she looked up to the place she'd been trying to reach on the concrete stairs, there was no one there.

All of the girls had gone, and the blond girl who'd fallen was also gone.

"Mommy?" she heard Emma say.

Emma was standing there beside Diana, looking from Diana's face to the sky.

"What are you looking at, Mommy?"

Asleep on the air mattress on her friend's floor, she dreams she's buying peaches again from the old Mexican couple in the country.

This time her friend isn't with her.

The old woman stands behind the old man, and her black shawl flaps in the breeze. Overhead, crows are circling the rusty pickup truck, but they don't scream.

The old man weighs, on a silver balance, the peaches she's picked out. He places them one by one on the scales, then he looks up at her angrily.

It's not until then that she notices that on the other scale, weighed against the fruit she wants, there's a baby.

A baby no larger than her hand.

It's bloody and naked, and it opens its mouth, but instead of a cry, what comes out is the screaming of a crow.

THE THUNDERSTORM OF THE EARLIER PART OF THE day had brought new life to everything—a steamy, groping greenness.

Flowers that had put off blooming—roses, rhododendrons—had bloomed with sticky brilliance as the day went on. In their heaviness, their sudden fullness, they seemed out of place, as if they'd arrived at the lawn party too desperate and overdressed. Like aging beauty queens. The air, humid and thick with their perfume, made Diana feel as if she might choke. She told Emma to roll her window up, and Diana turned the air-conditioning on.

"Who was that girl who fell?" she asked.

"I don't know," Emma said, and she shrugged. She was looking at her hands in her lap, not at Diana.

"Did you see her?" Diana asked.

Emma shrugged again. "I guess," she said. "I don't know."

"The girls were running right past her. No one was going to help."

"She was okay," Emma said. "She didn't need help."

Diana looked sharply at Emma and snapped, "I don't like that tone of voice, young lady."

Her daughter's rosebud mouth fell open, and she flushed, then muttered something under her breath and turned away from Diana.

But Diana reached over and took Emma's chin in her hand. "Look at me," she said.

Reluctantly Emma allowed her face to be turned toward her mother's.

"Listen, Emma, I don't want my daughter to be the kind of brat who won't stop to help a little girl who's fallen down. Do you hear me?"

Emma struggled to get away from Diana's grip.

"Do you hear me?" Diana asked again, more harshly.

"I hear you!" Emma said, and burst into tears. "I didn't! It wasn't my fault she fell down. I don't even know her. I wasn't anywhere *near* her!"

Diana let her daughter struggle free. She put her hand back on the steering wheel. "I know," she said, calming down, breathing deeply, but Emma continued to sob. Diana let her. She drove.

On the windshield a wand of light passed back and forth, changing colors as they slipped under the trees and telephone lines. Now blue, now pink, now green. Diana tried not to watch it in front of her. She knew she needed to keep her eyes on the road, not on the hypnotic sunlight on the glass. She glanced out the driver's side window at the sidewalk, where she saw a sparrow fluttering in a puddle. It must have been bathing, unless it was injured, drowning. It was gray, dull, and soft, like a dirty star.

They were already half a block past the sparrow in the puddle when Diana felt her breath leave her body again—an exhalation that felt as if the air had been yanked from her lungs.

That sparrow. How long had it been since she'd seen a sparrow? How long had it been since she'd seen *any* bird?

She inhaled hard and fast, catching the breath back, but she felt weak and dizzy with it. The air-conditioning was brutally cold inside her body, and it entered her like the realization that she had, somehow, forgotten about *birds.*

Where had they been?

Until that moment, that sparrow in the puddle, she hadn't seen a bird in . . . how long?

Surely they hadn't *all* gone south for the winter, come back late.

But where had they been? Why hadn't she thought of birds until this moment—birds in the backyard, birds on the phone lines, birds perched on the roof of the garage?

Surely she'd seen birds, but as hard as she tried she couldn't remember the last . . . when the *hell* was the last time she'd seen a bird?

Diana rubbed her eyes and again felt the place where the sharp wind and mirror of the minivan had grazed her, a place where she felt no pain whatsoever.

It was a mistake. Birds were everywhere. They had been all along. Now that the idea of them had returned to her, she saw them on the electrical wire, dashing through the air. She could hear them singing in the trees. A robin hopped along the sidewalk mechanically, like a parody of a robin. It had been precisely at the moment that Diana had noticed that birds were missing that the world had filled up with birds again.

Cold

When Emma had quit crying, Diana put a hand on her daughter's knee and said, "Let's go have an ice-cream cone. It seems like ice-cream-cone weather to me."

Emma nodded, but she didn't look at her mother and didn't smile.

Diana parked the car in front of Baskin Robbins, and they went inside.

Behind the ice-cream counter, there was a boy with red hair and freckles. To Diana he looked like a caricature of a teenage boy working at an ice-cream parlor. When she was a teenager herself, this was exactly the kind of boy she would have despised—too cute, too clean, too polite. She'd preferred boys who didn't smile, who didn't work. She'd preferred boys with a bit of the devil in them. Boys with tattoos. Motorcycles.

But then she'd changed.

And now she *loved* this boy.

She loved the freckles, and the eagerness with which he smiled and said, "Hi. How can I help you?"

And she loved the ice cream behind the glass—such a pure and simple pleasure!

Emma stood on tiptoe and put her face against the glass, peering in at it, and the boy watched her patiently. He *radiated* patience, kindness. He was wearing a white apron over his red T-shirt and jeans, and the apron was immaculately clean.

Diana didn't need to look. She knew exactly what she'd have. The same thing she always had. "A scoop of vanilla in a sugar cone, please," she said.

The boy smiled. He said, "We're out of vanilla, ma'am."

"Out of vanilla?" she asked.

He was still smiling. Was Diana mistaken, or did he seem to be making fun of her? Did he seem to be laughing to himself as he smiled at Diana?

"French vanilla?" Diana asked. "Vanilla yogurt. Soft-serve vanilla? Nothing?"

The smile stayed, but it grew thinner. His eyes were very pale and cold, as transparent as the glass between Diana and the ice cream. He *was* laughing at her. "No vanilla," he said.

Diana felt a hot flush of blood spread from her chest to her neck, and she stepped away from the boy, away from the counter.

"Emma," she said, "what do you want?"

"Blue Moon, please," Emma said to the boy, "in a cup, please."

"One scoop or two?" the boy asked Emma sweetly.

"One scoop, please," Emma said.

The boy looked from Emma back to Diana, and he was no longer smiling.

"Nothing for you, ma'am?"

Diana shook her head.

She looked away from him. In the glass, she could see her own reflection, and it was without substance, or dust. It was as clean and transparent, itself, as glass...

Without flesh, without wrinkles, without details, she looked like a girl again to herself, the kind of girl who'd taunted boys like the one who was taunting her now.

And on the other side of her own face, she could see the tubs of ice cream lined up cold and waiting for other customers. She saw that the one labeled VANILLA was utterly empty behind the glass.

It's the birds that wake the girls, scratching and singing outside on the sill and in the trees right outside the window....

Pigeons, sparrows, robins, and other birds whose names the girls don't know.

The sun is very yellow...a garish yellow, the yellow of a school bus. It bounces around on the shiny spoonlike surfaces of the leaves. Even with the shades pulled, it's too bright to sleep with those spoonfuls of yellow light in the room.

The girls get up, and each one tucks her own mussed hair behind her ears and rubs her eyes. They go to the kitchen in the oversized T-shirts they've slept in and drink Sunny Delight and eat yogurt, granola bars, Cap'n Crunch, and whatever else there is to eat that doesn't need to be cooked.

One of the girls tells the other about her dream.

The fruit.

The baby.

The old man and woman.

The abortion.

She doesn't mean to tell her friend about the abortion. It just slips out. She's never told anyone about the abortion. Suddenly it's real, and she starts to cry.

Not loudly. No sobbing. She keeps eating her Cap'n Crunch as she cries. The sugary milk in her cereal bowl tastes like tears. Her friend, the one who is a virgin, who has a bumper sticker on her car that says IT'S NOT A CHOICE, IT'S A CHILD, stands up and walks to the other side of the table, puts her arms around her, and holds her tightly until the one who is crying lets her spoon slip soundlessly into the milk.

EMMA'S LIPS WERE BLUE, BUT SHE LOOKED HAPPY WHEN she'd finished her ice cream.

They walked back to the minivan together and got in.

"I forgot to tell you," Diana said, trying to sound more cheerful than she felt. "I think we might have a new cat."

"What?" Emma said, then squealed and looked at Diana with wide astonished eyes. Diana had to look away from her blue lips.

"Yep," she said. "I think a cat found us today."

"What kind of cat? Mommy! Can we keep it?"

"Well," Diana said, "it's a shorthaired black cat—"

"Like Timmy!"

"Just like Timmy. And...if no one comes looking for him, I don't see why we shouldn't keep him."

"Yes! Yes!" Emma cried, clapping her hands.

They turned the corner onto Maiden Lane.

"Does Daddy know?" Emma asked.

"I called Daddy and told him this afternoon."

"Does Daddy say it's okay if we keep the cat?'

Diana glanced over at her daughter knowingly and said, "What do *you* think, Emma-o."

Emma smiled.

It was a joke between them: *Daddy says yes if Mommy wants him to.*

But just as Diana glanced over at her daughter—the blue against her pink lips had turned them to a kind of deep magenta, a parody of painted lips, the lipstick of a whore on Emma's sweet mouth, or a terrible death mask, the face of the child found floating in the neighbor's pool—a bird flew fast and hard into the driver's side window. Diana only saw it out of the corner of her eye. A black, feathered fist knocking once, then dropping into the road.

Instinctively she swerved, and the front tire of the minivan ran up over the curb, then thudded back down into the road when she corrected. Diana's chest hit the steering wheel, but it didn't hurt. Just a light punch that didn't knock the air out of her this time. Emma was bounced, but her seatbelt held her in place.

"Jesus," Diana said. She could feel springs underneath them, softening the jolt.

Emma said nothing. She had her hands folded tightly in her lap as if she were ready to say a prayer.

"Did you see that?" Diana asked.

"What?" Emma asked. She didn't look at Diana.

"A bird flew into the window."

Emma raised her shoulders and shook her head but didn't unclasp her hands.

Diana pulled slowly, with exaggerated care, into the driveway, past the front porch and the empty white rockers, then past Paul's bicycle, which had slipped into the daisies from the place where he'd propped it against the house. She parked the minivan outside the garage. She was shaking. She could hardly see in the bright afternoon sunlight. She didn't want to risk scraping the side of the minivan against the garage walls, something that was hard enough not to do when she was feeling fine and seeing clearly.

Emma jumped out quickly.

"Daddy?" she called to air.

Diana got out slowly, then went over to her husband's fallen bicycle and pulled it up by the handlebars. A mass of daisies, caught in the chain and spokes of the front tires, came with it, ripped up by their roots. The noise sounded like hair being torn out, and Diana felt sick and regretful at the sound of it. She let the bicycle fall back into the daisies.

"Hi, little miss blue lips," Paul said, stepping out of the garage. There was a rag in his hands.

"Daddy!" Emma cried, and threw herself into his arms.

He patted her hair.

Diana looked over at the two of them, at her husband's dirty hand in the gold silk of her daughter's hair...

"Don't," she said sharply. "You'll get it in her hair."

Paul took his hand off Emma's head and let it hover just above her. He looked at Diana. Then, full of false cheer, he said to Emma, "Sweetie-pie, can you go inside for a few minutes? I have to talk to Mommy."

Emma looked reluctant, but she went. The screen door slammed behind her lightly.

Paul stepped over to where Diana stood beside the daisies. He looked as though he might touch her, but he didn't.

What was it about him that she was, even now, so thoroughly and physically in love with?

The arms—which were muscular, but not overly so?

The beard, which grew grayer every year?

The eyes? They were blue, but so were her own, so were so many other eyes. She had seen many other pairs of blue eyes in her life.

But even the first time she saw him, his blue eyes might as well have been the first ones she'd ever seen. She felt she'd seen them before, that she'd dreamed them into being.

Philosophy 360: Medieval Sources of Modern Thought.

In it they'd read St. Augustine's *Confessions,* Apuleius, some Dante, some Boethius and Aquinas, *The Song of Roland, Beowulf*...

Diana had understood almost nothing.

She'd been a freshman in a class full of seniors, an art major in a class full of literature majors. She'd stumbled into registering for the class because her mother had told her she thought Professor McFee was the best teacher in the philosophy department. Her mother even confessed that she had a crush on him, but Professor McFee was many years younger than her mother, and married.

In class Diana had taken notes dizzily, trying to listen to Paul's lectures as she jotted down scraps of what he said. But she couldn't do both, couldn't listen and take notes at the same time. Finally she quit taking notes.

The lectures were delivered quickly, casually. He occasionally glanced at a yellow legal pad, but the lectures never seemed planned. He never wrote on the board. He never seemed to be talking directly about whatever it was they were studying at the time—but about, instead, the myriad issues that arose *out* of it.

Diana supposed this was the modern-thought part of the medieval sources, but she knew nothing about the Middle Ages and, oddly, even less about modern culture—at least not the modern culture in which Professor McFee and the other students seemed to be living, a culture full of foreign films and experimental novels and surrealist poets.

But every once in a while some piece of what was discussed reached out to her, lifted her, as if she were an injured person lying on her back . . . a hand at the back of her neck, repositioning her head, which would change her perspective entirely. . . .

"Sin?" he'd asked. "What is sin? What is evil? What does St. Augustine tell us about sin and about evil?"

No one raised a hand.

St. Augustine, she remembered from the reading, had committed one. As a boy he and another boy had stolen peaches from an orchard. They'd picked as much fruit from the trees as they could, and then they'd thrown the fruit away.

"Why did the boys steal the peaches?"

"Because they wanted the peaches?"

"No," someone answered, "they threw the peaches away."

"Exactly. They stole the peaches simply to be sinful. *That* is St. Augustine's definition of evil."

Her eyes had opened. It was as if she'd been very thirsty and been given a sip of cold water through a straw.

But most of the time in that class she felt as if she were standing between the Middle Ages and modern thought, trying to watch a movie that was being projected directly onto her face. Luckily they'd begun sleeping together before the midterm, which she never took, and by the end of the semester he'd left his wife and she'd moved into the apartment he'd rented for them at the edge of town.

Still, Diana kept her notes, what there had been of them before she'd quit trying to jot them down—a souvenir—and sometimes she'd take them off the bookshelf in her studio, where she kept them, and looked at them and wondered what it was she'd been trying to capture from Paul's lectures, in her strained, girlish writing. Some days she had even taken notes in pink ink....

"Can I buy you a cup of coffee?" he'd asked.

Each soul is a mystery only penetrable by God.

They'd crossed the street from Angel Hall to a coffee shop where candy was sold by the pound... cappuccino, cucumber sandwiches.

Diana wasn't a coffee drinker yet, so he bought her a bag of toffee and a cup of hot chocolate. A few days later, in her dorm room, his hands had shaken as he tried to unbutton her blouse, and finally she had to do it herself. Then, Professor McFee dropped to his knees and kissed her nipples, her torso, the firm muscles of her stomach, her belly button... he laughed at her gold ring there... and then he unzipped her jeans and slipped them down to her knees, kissed the rose at her hip.

Diana lay back on the single bed in her dorm room, which was decorated with stuffed animals and posters of ballet dancers, and as he slid the blouse completely off her shoulders and down her arms, he asked if she was a virgin.

"Yes," Diana said, and suddenly she was.

August is the awful, smothering sister of July....

Even the air-conditioning in their mothers' apartments can't keep August out of their beds at night. It slows down their blood. They don't want to go downtown because of the hot wet blanket of air in the streets. The stink of it. The fat hand of it across their mouths.

But they also don't want to find themselves alone in the mall again, wandering through the ridiculous echoes of it.

HOTTEST SUMMER ON RECORD, the headlines say.

One of the girls can see the backyards of her neighbors from her mother's sliding glass patio door. There's an aqua blue pool full of water down there. It shivers in the sunlight . . . watery ribbons like brain waves being measured on the surface.

The houses below her are empty all day.

No one swims in that pool.

There are no cars in the driveways.

She can see it all from behind the sliding glass.

"We could go to the public pool," the other one suggests from her end of the phone line.

"No way. All those little kids."

"But what if we get caught?"

"We'll get yelled at."

"I guess you're right. Nobody goes to jail for swimming in the neighbor's pool."

"ARE YOU OKAY?" PAUL ASKED. "I'VE BEEN WORRIED sick."

"I'm fine," Diana said, touching the place at her temple where the mirror had hit her. There was nothing there. Not even a tender spot. She was fine. She would be fine. The girl she thought she'd seen him walking with, the one with her hand tucked into his back pocket, now that she was here again, face-to-face with her husband, she knew she'd been wrong.

Lately she was often mistaken about what she'd seen and what was really there.

Hormones.

Or maybe her eyes. Maybe she needed not only sunglasses but *glasses.*

Maybe she should see a doctor.

Paul smiled as if he were relieved.

Then they heard the scream.

It came from the kitchen—a piercing wail—and they both ran toward it. Paul got to the screen door first, and the door slammed behind him before Diana reached it. For a moment she saw everything in the kitchen through the screen . . . all of it broken up into molecules, all of it made up of microscopic pieces that could have been taken apart by a physicist and exploded or rearranged.

Emma had dropped her Snow White backpack and was standing with her back to the kitchen counter. One hand was covering her mouth, and Diana could see her eyes. They were large and frightened.

"What?" Paul yelled, taking Emma by the shoulders and shaking her gently. He sounded more annoyed than concerned, Diana thought.

She hurried up behind him and pulled him away from Emma.

"Sweetheart, what's the matter?" Diana asked. She took the hand gently away from her daughter's mouth. Her lips were still blue.

Emma began to shake her head. "No," she said, and tears started in her eyes. "No, no, no."

She pointed to the water and food dishes Diana had left beside the refrigerator for the cat. Both dishes were empty.

"What?" Paul snapped, also looking at the dishes.

"I saw it," Emma said. She continued to shake her head. Her blond hair whisked in brilliant strands around her face. The sun was low in the sky outside, preparing to set, and it streamed in through the kitchen window over the sink and lit up each hair on Emma's head and also illuminated the billion specks of dust that swirled around them always, usually invisible—the galaxies and universes that surrounded them all the time, the vast stretches of stars amid which they breathed and ate without noticing at all.

"It's not Timmy," Emma said. She began to sob and then sank to the floor, crossed her legs, and buried her face in her hands. She rocked back and forth, lit up from behind and surrounded by so many dry little stars, and wailed louder.

Paul got down on the kitchen floor and pulled Emma's hands away from her face, then pulled her to her feet. Emma swung an arm at him, which hit him squarely in the chest. He held more tightly to her shoulders, and then she started to kick.

"It's not Timmy!" she screamed. "Get it *out* of here. Get it *out* of here!"

"Of course it's not Timmy," Paul shouted over her screaming. "Timmy's dead. It's just another black stray."

He dropped Emma's shoulders and turned, narrowing his eyes at Diana accusingly. "Did you tell her that the cat was *Timmy*?"

"No," Diana said defensively. "Of course I didn't tell her—"

The cat sauntered into the kitchen then, looking at them calmly, unmoved by the commotion, and glanced down at its empty dishes.

Emma cringed and covered her eyes with her hands again, screaming, "Get it *out* of here."

Then, as if to taunt her, the cat padded across the kitchen floor to Emma, bowed its glossy head, and rubbed its ears against her ankle socks.

Emma opened her mouth, and this time nothing came out. She sagged a little. She looked down at the animal rubbing its face on the top of her feet, at her ankles. It was purring wetly, and Diana thought Emma was calming down, that she was seeing the cat for what it was, or wasn't...

But then she sank entirely, mouth still open, blue lips parted, dropping to the kitchen floor, and such a terrible cry came from so deep inside of her that Diana had to cover her ears.

Dust

Beside her in the dark Paul could have been anyone.

She could have been anyone.

She'd changed the sheets after dinner, so there wasn't even the familiar smell of their bodies. Instead there was the scent of fabric softener, powdered flowers. Paul turned the light back on beside the bed and said, "Diana, we have to talk."

Diana reached across his body and turned the light back off.

"Diana," he protested.

"We don't need the light on to talk," she said.

Paul sank back into his pillow. In front of her eyes Diana saw flaming cups and saucers where the lamplight had branded stuttering images of itself on her retinas as she'd blinked into it.

She closed her eyes and they appeared on her eyelids... burning cups and saucers drifting backward into a dark garden of powdered flowers.

A hellish tea party, a tea party in hell.

"About today...," Paul started. "Did you see the girl—?"

He interrupted himself. Diana said nothing. The bedroom windows were open. It was a warm night, full moon. As her eyes adjusted to the darkness she could see the moonlight sifting into their room through the window screen. The sheer white curtains had turned to ephemeral pillars in the stillness, filled with moonlight. From her studio where she'd shut him up for the night with his food and water, Diana could hear Timmy yowling to get out. It was a cat's kind of night—balmy, bright, full of shadows and whispers and the smell of catnip in the breeze.

"No," Diana said.

Paul inhaled. She couldn't tell if it was an inhalation of despair or of frustration.

"Well," he said, "I just didn't want you to think—"

"I didn't," Diana said.

Outside their bedroom window she thought she heard something like footsteps in high grass, but the grass outside the window wasn't high.

It sounded like a horse eating hay, or a scythe in the daisies. But when Diana listened more closely, she realized it was just her husband, he'd already fallen asleep—his familiar steady breath beside her.

They know as soon as they slip into it—the clean kiss of chlorine, the silence of the neighborhood in the middle of the afternoon—that it's the right thing to be doing, the only thing to be doing at this moment in their lives.

The water seems to be made of silk and brilliance. They've never felt more naked, as if they've slipped not only out of their clothes but out of their *skins.*

At first the girls splash and laugh, and then they grow silent. They float past one another slowly on their backs.

One of them dives under, and the other watches her smooth flash under the water—blue, then blindingly white.

IT HAD BEEN YEARS SINCE DIANA HAD FOUND HERSELF lying awake through the night, and it surprised her to realize that the night wasn't quiet. How, she wondered to herself, had she *ever* slept through one... all the noises outside the house, and in it, above her, below her, on every side—*inside* her—as if the darkness were *made* of sound.

Little wings against the window screens, animal feet in the grass, the faraway sound of a train—no whistling, just locomotion and a rusty rumbling—and beyond that, the freeway, the steady sound of tires and wind over tar. Someone drove down Maiden Lane in a car with bad brakes. As it came to a stop at the end of the block, there was a terrible screeching. And beyond that, the sound of people still awake in their houses all up and down the block, and the cumulative sound of block after block of people sleeping and awake. Blow-dryers, televisions, laughter, snoring... it rose above Briar Hill as an undulating veil of white noise, and dispersed, then fell back to earth, some of it wafting away on the breeze, and some of it slipping through the window screen into the bedroom, which had its own noises—Paul's breathing, the settling of the floor—as did Diana's body. Heartbeat. Blood. Breath. She swallowed, and even the sound of that would have been enough to wake her if she'd been asleep.

And behind all of it, Timmy...

Yowling.

Timmy, angry in the darkness, scratching at the studio door with his claws, locked up and wanting to get out.

How long had it been since she'd found herself lying awake all night?

Insomnia . . . like *birds.* She had forgotten about insomnia. What else had she forgotten to add to the world as she observed it in middle age, in this strange threshold in which she found herself waiting now? Crickets?

Crickets.

The second she remembered crickets, they were back. The incredible electric hum of them in the summer night. The trilling rhythm of them filling up the whole night as if night were a terrible machine made out of a million insects, all calling to one another with their wings.

Diana sat up.

The sound of the crickets drowned out everything else, even the sound of her own breathing.

The sound of the crickets *was* the sound of everything else. How had she forgotten them, or where had they gone, where had *it* gone—the whole lifetime of summer nights filled up with the trilling of crickets? Of *insects*?

Butterflies . . .

Surely she'd remembered butterflies. She knew she'd seen one the other afternoon. Emma had chased a black one out of the yard. Butterflies were insects—although when she was four years old Emma had insisted that butterflies were flowers.

And moths.

Diana had heard moths outside the window screens before she remembered crickets. Before she'd remembered crickets she'd remembered moths and hadn't even realized that she'd forgotten them, the thin filaments of their bodies, the way their wings seemed made of paper and also made of flesh.

And hadn't she seen a june bug clinging to the trunk of a tree in the front yard last summer? It had been brown and shiny, but when Diana looked more closely at it she could see that it was just a shell, a bug's shed skin. The june bug itself had crawled away and left a transparent amber self behind, still clinging.

But spiders; when was the last time she'd seen a spider? In her mother's apartment they used to make their ways somehow into the bathtub in the summer and climb the tile to the ceiling, sew webs in the corners of the shower walls.

And flies.

Flies had little razor-shaped wings and iridescent eyes.

And beetles, waddling along with their shells on their backs, cracking under her shoes whether she meant to step on them or not.

Hadn't Mr. McCleod told them once how many different kinds of insects there were in the world? Hadn't it been staggering, the number and variety—a number too large to comprehend and therefore impossible to file away in the mind?

Bees! She knew she'd seen bees. You couldn't remember roses and not remember bees.

You couldn't remember summer and not remember roses....

Paul rolled over and pulled the sheet and quilt with him, and Diana was left exposed to the darkness in her white summer nightgown, which looked so white in the moonlight that it seemed to be *made* of moonlight.

She got out of bed.

She'd go to her studio.

She might as well draw. There was no sense lying awake all night. Now she remembered insomnia.

They dry themselves and hurry back into their clothes, then run giggling down the strangers' driveway to the sidewalk, back into the wavering wall of heat that is an August afternoon.

Back to the apartment, where they eat Doritos and drink Seven-Up. The taste is sweetness and light, like water extracted with syringes from flowers.

The air-conditioning feels cooler now that they've been in the water and emerged from it. They turn the radio on. Jewel is singing a song that was popular a few years before...

"Who will save your soul?"

Her voice is like a length of silk thread taken up by a thin, bright needle.

One of the girls has goose bumps. They're both wearing spaghetti-strapped tops and cutoffs. The one who's cold pulls an afghan over her legs. It's something that her dead grandmother crocheted two decades before—olive green, forest green, and orange, with terrible geometric shapes all meeting in an ugly swirl at the center.

She's never liked the afghan, into which her mother sometimes sobs when she's missing her own dead mother.

The girl feels sad... the song... the cool water gone. Next year they'll be seniors, and then what? Where will they go? Who will they become?

As hard as she tries she can't imagine it:

Dormitories, pizzas, her mother's apartment empty of her. When she gets past graduation... wearing a black gown, like a witch or a nun, on the football field... she sees a yellow sign. It says YIELD, or NO OUTLET, or PED XING, and her imagination grinds to a halt.

She clears her throat and asks her friend, "Have you been baptized?"

"Sure," her friend says. "When I was a baby, but again when I was going to the Pentecostal church. We went on a retreat. Pastor Mallory baptized me in a little creek that ran through the woods where we were camping. It was just after I was born again."

Born again.

They've never talked about that. Though they've talked about sex, their periods, their fantasies, their fathers, all the secret painful things, they've really never talked about God. No one ever really talked about God. A whole lifetime could pass by, and God would never be mentioned, or death.

From behind the pulled shades there's a hot breath sneaking through the imperceptible spaces between the windows and their frames.

IT WAS LARGE, THE NIGHT.

It seemed to be empty, but as soon as she turned on the back porch light, hundreds of moths swarmed out of the darkness and began to circle the bulb.

Where had they been before she turned on the light? What had they been doing until then?

They thrummed dully against one another with their dusty little wings made of—what?

A kind of skin like toilet tissue, the same thinness that covered every living thing, the thin film that existed between the earth and the sky, one moment and the next. What else?

Diana stepped into it, the night, closing the door quietly behind her so as not to wake up Paul or Emma.

As soon as the house was behind her, she felt calm again. The grass was dry but cool on her bare feet. She could smell roses. It was quiet...

The noises that had kept her awake were still there, but they were muffled by the enormity of the world. The sky, black but full of stars—she looked directly up at the Little Dipper, which was like a spoonful of diamond dust—was high, unfathomably high. Plenty of room for everything.

She looked from the sky to the backyard.

Emma's plastic pony was shining whitely in the night.

Diana felt it return her gaze with its blank eyes. It seemed ready to say something... something Diana knew she wouldn't want to hear. All the years that the thing had spent outside staring into the side of the garage, the weather, the night, the nothing. It couldn't move, and it couldn't disintegrate. Made of plastic, it would last forever.

What would *forever* mean to something without brain waves, or respiration?

Forever. An eternity of insomnia. Diana looked back at the pony, and—a trick of the eye—in its contrast to the darkness, it seemed to move.

She looked away, stepping out of its line of vision. She hurried over to the garage and rolled up the door, which groaned like a stone being rolled from a cave. A hot breath exhaled from it, smelling of gasoline, and Diana walked through it, the cement slab strangely cold against the soles of her bare feet, and she climbed the stairs to her studio.

From behind the door Timmy must have heard her coming, because he'd quit yowling. Now he was purring.

Diana could sense his impatience. He wanted out of there, whether it was safe and full of places to sleep and food to eat or not. The second she opened the door Timmy dashed past her, down the stairs, and out of the garage. A soft darkness hurrying out to join the larger, softer darkness.

By the end of August, the hot wet blanket of humidity that's been lying over Briar Hill for two weeks finally lifts.

One of the girls has been given a car by her father, who's moving to California with his wife and son. It has no air-conditioning, so they keep the windows rolled down, and their hair is ratted and wild by the time they get wherever they're going.

It's ending quickly.

Summer.

Soon they'll be back behind their desks—the smell of Pine-Sol on the shiny surfaces—staring into Michael Patrick's or Mary Olivet's back.

They take the car to the zoo.

Why not?

Who says teenage girls can't go to the zoo?

One of them hasn't been there since she was a child, holding her father's hand as he pushed the stroller of his newer child and talked to his newer wife. She remembered only the hand, the way it kept slipping out of hers when he had to readjust the direction of the stroller he was pushing... that and a lion sprawled out on a rock, yawning, lifting its lazy head up to look at her, then dropping back into its nap.

The other girl had come to the zoo the summer before with an older man who kept exotic pets. He bored her with facts about wolves and lynxes and bought her a snow cone. The animals seemed to recognize him, she thought. In the snake house he put his hand up her shirt when no one was looking. He kissed her hard enough to make her lower lip bleed, near the monkey pit. She was already pregnant, although she didn't know it then.

Near the lion's den she'd seen Mrs. Adams, who'd been her third-grade teacher. Mrs. Adams had been hugely pregnant then, and Mrs. Adams was hugely pregnant now. She was pushing an empty stroller, waddling, and though she didn't seem to recognize her, Mrs. Adams looked disapprovingly at the teenage girl holding the hand of an older man.

Today the zoo is crawling with children.

They shout and scramble as their mothers and fathers, looking weary and washed-out in the bright light, hurry after. The parents are carrying things, pushing things.

The girls are wearing short shorts and have put temporary tattoos on their ankles.

The fathers of the children look at the tattoos while their wives and children look at the polar bear, who is pacing back and forth along the moat between himself and the zoo visitors, with blood on the white fur around his mouth.

The girls know, moving through the zoo, that they are closer in kind to the children than to anything else there....

The animals are nothing like the girls. Dulled, pacing, or swimming in circles in their dreamless sleep.

And neither are the adults, with their diaper bags and other burdens.

The girls, like the children, have to hold their stomachs because they're laughing so hard. They want treats—snow cones, candy corn, licorice whips. They are still like children, except that the world, in all of its complexity and implications, is coming into focus for them:

The hungry boredom of the polar bear, like the fathers; the effect of their own flesh on the mothers who follow their husbands' glances in the direction of the girls, then look away.

They aren't children. Or animals, or women. Briefly they're in a state between each of these. They are all of these things at once.

DIANA WOKE UP AT HER DESK WITH HER FACE IN THE crook of her arm, which was sprawled across a piece of blank drawing paper.

Timmy, who'd stayed outside for only a few minutes before climbing the stairs to her study and scratching to get back in, stood up from the braided rug where he'd slept. He stretched, then sat on his haunches and stared at Diana simply. No affection. No judgment. He was just looking.

The sun was coming up. The smeared peach and gold of it lit up the curtains on the window of her studio. It could only have been about six o'clock in the morning, but Diana heard voices, and she stood up and stretched, and was surprised that she wasn't stiff from having fallen asleep sitting up. She felt well. Oddly rested. She went to the window and parted the curtains, which seemed to be *made* of dawn, lit up as they were with new sun. She looked out.

They were back.

The blond and her boyfriend had come back to the Ellsworths' swimming pool.

The girl was sitting at the edge of it, naked, dangling her bare feet in the water, which was plum colored in the shade of the Ellsworths' house and the sun just coming up. With one hand she was rubbing the back of her own neck, and in the other she held a joint, which she brought to her lips, inhaled from it deeply. Diana could taste it in her own lungs . . . the sweetness, just like *dawn . . . pollen, flower petals, the smell of the baking supplies aisle, fruit cocktail, sun.*

She held the smoke in her lungs for a minute and then exhaled, but Diana could see nothing escape, not even a plume of it, from the girl, who continued a conversation with her boyfriend. He was floating on his back. Diana couldn't quite make out what she was saying.

So I was . . . anatomy, and he was, like, get your scalpel, there's the sweetheart; don't put your hand on that.

This time their nakedness didn't shock Diana. She'd seen their bodies before. The slick perfection of them. The shocking youth of them. The boy let out a loud laugh at what she'd said, then sank out of sight—only the waxy vagueness of him under the plum-colored water from where Diana watched—a moving smoothness, like a dolphin, or a cadaver. Then he resurfaced between the girl's legs.

He shook his head to get the water out of his eyes, then put his face there, between her legs.

She tossed what was left of the joint into the Ellsworths' pool, then spread her legs farther, inched to the edge of the pool, and leaned backward.

Before Diana had thought about it, she'd yanked open the window and was shouting through the screen, "What's going on over there? What are you kids doing?"

The boy splashed backward but came up again quickly, sputtering and shaking his head. The girl stood up and looked straight at Diana, and she called up, "Fuck you, you old bag."

The boy burst into laughter then and pulled himself up the side of the pool in one muscular movement, and then he ran to a towel hanging over one of the Ellsworths' lounge chairs. He tied the towel around his waist, grabbed his clothes, and ran, still laughing, behind the Ellsworths' toolshed.

At least he was ashamed, Diana thought.

But the girl just put her hand on her hip and stared straight up into the window of Diana's studio.

It scared her, the boldness, but there was nothing Diana could do now but face it. She had to say something. She said, "Do the Ellsworths know what you've been up to?"

The girl narrowed her eyes and smirked.

"We *are* the Ellsworths," she said.

Steam

Diana trembled in the shower.

Though the water was scalding hot and sending up scarves and veils of steam, fogging the shower doors and everything beyond them—though her skin stung from the burning and she could see that her hands and feet were red from it—she couldn't get warm. The cold was too deep inside her. She needed...what? Hot cocoa? Tea? Whiskey? Something that could get to *that* coldness.

We are *the Ellsworths....*

Diana had pulled the curtains closed and hurried across her studio to the door. When Timmy tried to follow her, she pushed him back gently with one bare foot. In the garage she'd stumbled on the handle of a rake, which was propped upside down, leaning against a beam, and it had fallen on her with its claws. It had drawn blood on her neck and left its paw swipe there.

She was holding her neck in the darkness of the garage when she saw a silhouette standing in the open doorway, someone blacked out by the sun still rising behind him.

"Diana."

Before she recognized the voice—which was husky, insistent, the voice of someone trying to wake her from a very deep sleep, from an ocean of sleep, trying to call her back to the surface or pull her out from underneath the million shining windowpanes of a coma—she screamed.

And the screaming had been like a cold wind, like a cold broom inside her, sweeping her out, a whole blizzard kicked up by a whisk broom, a deep coldness that even now in the burning shower she couldn't reach.

"Diana," he'd said, and taken her by the shoulders and shaken her harder than he needed to . . . was she still screaming?

"Diana! Stop it; stop it!"

She could smell wolf. Clean fur and blood on his breath. Snow White in her glass coffin, devoured by a wolf . . .

No, that was Little Red Riding Hood.

He'd pressed his whiskered muzzle next to her ear and whispered softly, "It's okay. It's okay. It's okay . . ."

Paul.

Her hand, which she'd pressed to her neck, came away with three stripes of blood across the palm. She held it to his face, which was gentle with sadness. He wasn't going to kiss her back to life or eat her like a wolf. This wasn't a fairy tale. How could she have forgotten—as she had forgotten birds, forgotten crickets, forgotten sleeplessness—that this, too, came with middle age?

The braided daughter . . . the clapboard house . . . the handsome husband.

But how could she have forgotten all the rest?

All those years, all those men walking through the zoos and parks and malls holding the hands of their wives while they looked at the legs of the girls walking by.

Of course, he was going to leave her for a younger woman. *How could she have forgotten?*

And then she'd started to cry, a pure glare filling up her eyes, a brightness like rhinestones or water glistening on the far edge of the horizon, and he held her.

"It's okay," he said again.

But why was she crying?

What was she grieving?

The boy moving between the girl's legs with his mouth, with his tongue?

The sun rising behind them?

Her dream life full of cups and curtains, furniture, appliances, walls?

Her daughter's golden braids?

Her husband's cool blue eyes?

Summer, full of roses?

"Stop," he said, patting her on the back.

But she couldn't stop. Though it was all still there—the minivan, the rake, the garden, the plastic pony, the dream house, which contained her dreams as well as her things—it was going to be over. She could smell it on him. Her husband was in love with a younger woman . . . a girl. She'd known it. They'd told her . . .

If he'll leave his wife for you, someday he'll leave you for . . .

Who?

A student?

Or was the girl she'd seen him with even younger than a college student? A girl just out of high school? *In* high school? A girl who'd seen him walking across the commons . . . a girl he'd seen . . . toffee and a cup of hot chocolate because she was so young she didn't drink coffee . . . a girl he'd glimpsed, and who'd stolen him, as Diana had, with her youth, her fresh beauty?

Diana's eyes cleared. Over her husband's shoulder she could see the shadows of the trees in the sun coming up and how they projected black and orange tongues on the white clapboard of their house. She blinked, then looked at Paul, who looked old in the morning sun, like a man with fewer years ahead of him than he had behind him, like a man who, out of a desperate fear of death, had decided to leave his wife.

He held her weakly.

"It's the last day of school," Diana said. She pushed him away gently. "I have to take Emma and her friends to the zoo. I have to take a shower."

He let her go, nodding.

She said nothing else, and he never brought himself to say what it was he'd come to tell her. But in the shower, the coldness wouldn't wash away. When Diana stepped out of the shower, her skin prickled and the bathroom was full of steam, which she stepped into as if it were a cloud, or thought, or the future, and she wrapped a white towel around herself and looked in the mirror.

There was no reflection there until she'd wiped away a circle with her hand.

Then, in that circle, Diana saw her own face.

Flushed but familiar.

Aged, but *her face* . . . the face she wore when she was seventeen.

September comes.

One of the girls picks the other up in the morning on the first day of school. On the drive through Briar Hill, which glows fiercely under the purple velvet of the morning sky, they're quiet. Neither girl has been up this early in the morning since the beginning of June.

Briar Hill High looks the same, and utterly changed. The bricks look as if they've been washed, and the grassy slope on which it rests is so freshly cut that the tracks of the riding mower's wheels stand out brightly against the bristling green. The windows shine blankly... no fingerprints, no smudges, no dust. And the students climbing out of cars in the parking lot are wearing new clothes, looking around. The ghosts of those who graduated the year before are still there—Amanda Greenberg swinging her legs from the trunk of her father's BMW; Mark Twitchell, spitting on the sidewalk; Bob Blau, wearing a black sports coat and pink nail polish; Sandy Ellsworth, with her head bowed, taking one last drag from her joint, behind the wheel of her beat-up Thunderbird, her white blond hair full of electricity and light—but in less than a day they'll be gone.

"Oh my god," one of the girls says, "there's Nate."

She parks carefully but quickly between a Jeep and a black Buick Riviera.

"He *shaved* his *head.*"

They look at each other with opened mouths, then burst into laughter.

They look again.

"Jesus. Am I seeing things, or does he have a stud in his lower lip?"

"Yes!"

Again, they laugh. The car window is unrolled and Nate Witt, who's only a few yards away, turns to look in the direction of the laughter, and the stud in his lower lip catches light. The girls quickly swallow their laughter and wave politely at him.

He smiles . . . a dangerous, amazing smile.

Mayqueen.

It should have seemed like another lifetime, a century ago, but it didn't. She could still feel the precarious weight of the tiara on her head, held there with bobby pins stuck deeply, painfully, into her blond hair.

She'd worn Maureen's white dress, the one Diana had helped her choose at Prom World only a few weeks before. She'd had it taken in because Maureen was bustier than she was, but the dress hadn't been shortened, the length was just right. They'd been the same height.

"No," Diana had said, shaking her head. "I can't—"

But Maureen's mother had taken her by the shoulders and said, "*Please* . . . Do it for Maureen. I can't bury my daughter in her prom dress," and so Diana wore it.

She remembered how Mr. McCleod's hands trembled as he helped her onto the float, which was a mass—a surreal mass—of real and tissue-paper roses, some of which she and Maureen had made themselves at the kitchen table in her mother's apartment, some of which had been donated from florists all over the country, sent in memory of the victims and in honor of the survivors.

They shivered in the breeze.

A sigh rose from the bleachers as Diana stepped up.

"You're the most beautiful Mayqueen Briar Hill High has ever had," Mr. McCleod whispered to her...

The sky was perfectly, sharply blue, and the smell of the real and unreal roses drifted in a wave over the football stadium. Diana looked up, and the sun was so brilliant overhead it seemed to light up the very atoms and molecules between them and the rest of the universe—tiny rhinestones. When she looked out she saw her parents sitting next to each other in the bleachers.

Were they even holding hands?

Both of them were crying.

They'd handed the microphone to her, and Diana had let go of the string of white helium balloons she was holding in her hand, releasing them.

"These are for you, Maureen," she'd said, and they'd all looked up into the sun to watch them float through the air, lighter than the air, lighter than anything else in heaven or on Earth.

The linoleum is waxed, and its gold flecks are bright under the hundreds of pairs of new shoes hurrying to their first classes as the bell rings...

The sound of it is shockingly loud.

Had it always been that loud?

"Good luck," one of the girls says to the other. They have different first-hour classes, and they have to say good-bye.

Though they've only been best friends for half a year, it's hard to part in the hallway, to let go of the summer they've spent with each other. For weeks it will still *seem* like summer, but then the leaves will change and the sun will spin away, growing higher and lighter in the sky over Briar Hill.

It's hard to part in the hallway, to imagine one of them without the other in the world, taking notes, thinking thoughts, waiting for the bell to ring.

"See you at lunch,"one of the girls says wistfully to the other. Then she leans in and whispers, "You look awesome."

"So do you," the other says.

They hug each other briefly.

DIANA LEANED IN MORE CLOSELY TO HER REFLECTION IN the mirror.

But her reflection had become obscured by breath.

Still she looked unflinchingly at herself.

It was something she'd been proud of... proud that aging hadn't come to her as anguished change. She'd known the very moment she'd crossed over the threshold from maid to matron, and she'd done that, as she did this now, as bravely as she was able.

It hadn't been her wedding day, and it hadn't been when she'd had the baby. It was later. She'd been... what? Thirty-three? Thirty-four? She was driving to work, having just dropped Emma off at preschool. It was winter. A dusty snow was blowing its feather boas across the street. She'd pulled up to a four-way stop. Although there were no other cars at the intersection, there was a girl waiting there to cross the street.

A redhead. Probably about eighteen. A college student maybe, or a high school senior.

She was wearing a silver down jacket and headphones, and she was nodding and smiling to some music that only she could hear... a deeply secret smile, the smile of someone who was young, who'd never been anything but young. Before she stepped into the street, the girl looked up directly into the windshield at Diana, but her expression didn't change.

Surely their eyes had met, Diana thought. Diana thought she saw a faint flicker of recognition pass over the girl's face, but she was so deeply inside her own music, her own amusing thoughts, that Diana was nothing to her. *That was me,* Diana thought. *I was that girl once. I thought no one else had ever been that girl or ever would—*

The past tense surprised her. When she finally passed through that intersection, she was a mature woman.

She began soon after that to call her younger female students "Honey." She started wearing expensive blouses instead of bright colors. She threw away her small collection of ankle bracelets. She bought a one-piece bathing suit so that when she took Emma to the pool in the summer, no one would see the rose tattooed on her hip.

The mirror steamed again, and Diana let the white shadow of her own breath creep slowly across her face.

The cafeteria is deafening....

Silverware on the linoleum, quarters emptying into the vending machine's silver tray. Someone is pounding a table with a fist, and it sounds like a series of small explosions. The shrieking laughter of a girl. A boy making electric guitar sounds in his throat. Standing in the cafeteria line, Rita Smith, looking larger and more unpleasant than she had the year before, shouts, "Get that away from me," at a boy who's tossed a plastic black tarantula in her direction.

One of the girls slips quickly into the empty chair beside the other girl, who has been sipping chocolate milk from a tiny carton and waiting.

"You're not going to believe it," she says before she says hello. She looks into her friend's chocolate-milk carton. It looks sweet and dark in there, and a thirst for chocolate milk—*that* chocolate milk—rises in her. She looks away from it and says, "He's in my homeroom—"

Her friend looks up.

"Nate?" she asks.

"Nate," she answers. "He sits right next to me."

"No way! Get out of here!" her friend says. "Did you talk to him?"

She shrugs, smiles. "I said, 'I like your lip thing.'" She points to the place on her own lower lip.

"And what did he say?"

"He smiled."

"Nate *smiled*?"

"Nate smiled," she says.

WHEN DIANA CAME OUT OF THE BATHROOM AND WALKED barefoot through the hallway, still wrapped in a towel, she saw that Emma was sitting up in bed. She wasn't smiling.

"Where's that cat?" Emma asked.

Diana tried to smile. She said, "Honey, I put him in my studio for the night. There's no reason to be afraid of the cat."

Emma said nothing. But she looked as though she'd found out some secret of Diana's—had read her diary, had read her *mind*—and wasn't pleased, though she had new power because of it.

Emma said, "I want that cat to be *gone*."

Diana pretended not to have heard her and kept walking.

Part Five

Music

THE THREE GIRLS SAT IN THE BACKSEAT OF THE MINIVAN while Diana drove.

Sarah Ann Salerno was wearing a sundress and a little embroidered sweater over it. The sweater was white, and the roses were sewn with fat pink yarn all up and down the sleeves. It was, Diana thought, a very ugly sweater, but something someone had taken a great deal of trouble to make.

"I like your sweater, Sarah Ann," Diana said into the rearview mirror at a miniaturized reflection of the little girl.

"Thank you," Sarah Ann said.

"Did your grandma make it?"

"No," Sarah Ann said, putting her hands on the sleeves of the sweater as if to hide the roses from Diana. "My grandmother's dead," she said.

"So is mine!" Mary Olivet chimed in as if with good news.

"Mine, too," Emma said, and Diana inhaled in surprise before she remembered it . . . remembered her mother . . .

Before she had a chance to think any further, Emma began to sing—

"A little bit of Sarah in my life . . . a little bit of Mary by my side . . . a little bit of Emma all night long."

The other two girls began to sing along, and the sound of their thin voices, in unison, singing a song Diana only vaguely remembered having heard before made her feel . . . what? Woozy? Anxious?

She tried to listen to the words of the song as she drove the three girls down Roosevelt Avenue, which would take them directly to the zoo, but she found she couldn't listen to their singing and drive at the same time. She found herself gripping the steering wheel much harder than she needed to, harder than was safe . . . gripping the steering wheel so hard she couldn't steer.

The only other vehicle on Roosevelt Avenue that morning was an old station wagon, the kind of station wagon mothers used to drive when Diana was a child—paneled strangely, as if it had been intended to look like a den instead of a car. Her own mother hadn't owned one, but Diana could remember sitting in the backseat of such a station wagon, driven by another girl's mother, being taken to a movie or to a field trip to the zoo.

The girls went on and on with their song. It seemed to culminate in one lyric: *A little bit of——— is all I need.* A new girl's name was inserted every time. They sang out the names without hesitating, as if they knew exactly which names followed which. Diana glanced at them again in the rearview mirror.

Her daughter was in the middle. On her right was Sarah Ann Salerno, and on her left was Mary Olivet—who, Diana had to admit, was much prettier than either of the other girls.

Mary had black ringlets that fell almost to her waist, and which looked like an artist's romanticized vision of a little girl's ringlets. Her eyes were olive green and enormous, dark-lashed. Her lips seemed naturally, though strangely, red...

And her teeth were perfectly straight and dazzlingly white against her somewhat dusky skin.

Diana looked hard at the little girl singing in her backseat. Mary Olivet. Diana only looked away from her to be sure there were no cars pulling out or slowing down in front of her.

That beauty...

Whose beauty was that?

She recognized something in the girl that reminded her of...who?

"Mary?" she asked.

"Yes, Mrs. McFee?" Mary responded politely.

"Have I ever met your mom?"

"I don't think so," Mary said.

"What's your mom's name?"

Diana knew the answer before it came.

"Amanda," Mary said.

"Amanda Greenberg?" Diana asked.

"Yeah!" Mary said. "That was her name before my daddy!"

"I knew her in high school," Diana said. "You look—"

The station wagon with the pine paneling slowed down in front of the minivan, and then it came to a stop, and Diana slowed behind it, though she couldn't see any reason for the station wagon's stopping. They were in the middle of the road. There were no traffic lights, no stop signs, no other cars.

Diana pulled the minivan all the way up to the station wagon's bumper. There was nothing where the license plate should have been. She was just about to honk when the girls began to sing again... "A little bit of Diana's all I need... A little bit of Amanda's all I need—"

"Girls!" Diana shouted over their singing. "That's enough. Sing a different song if you're going to sing."

Behind her they went quiet for a moment. The station wagon ahead still hadn't moved. Diana considered swerving around it to the right, but that would have meant driving up onto the curb with the minivan. There was no shoulder here. And she was afraid to pull around the station wagon to the left, even though no cars were coming in the opposite lane, because she didn't feel she could be certain that the driver of the station wagon wasn't planning to make a left-hand turn and had, perhaps, no turn signal with which to indicate it.

Finally Diana honked.

The huge noise of it startled her, and she felt embarrassed... apologetic. Behind her the girls began to sing again. It seemed spontaneous, yet they'd all three begun at the same time, singing even more loudly than before, as if to irk Diana.

"A little bit of Sandy's all I need... A little bit of Maureen's all I need..."

It was, Diana realized suddenly, a song that had been popular when Diana was in high school, though the girls had altered the lyrics, substituting new names for the ones that had been in the old song.

How long had it been since Diana had heard that song, and where had the girls learned it? Diana had a vivid memory of being in the passenger seat, beside Maureen, with that song on the radio in the morning on the way to school. They were singing along, but as they got closer to the school, they lost reception and had to sing without the radio.

Listening to the girls now, it seemed to Diana at that moment that the song she'd been singing twenty-two years ago with her friend in her friend's car was the last song she'd heard in...

How long?

How long since she'd heard...not just this song, but *any* song?

How long since she'd heard *music*? *Surely*—

She felt frightened... the headache. She put her hand to her temple and honked the horn again impatiently, holding it down harder and longer this time than the time before. Still the station wagon didn't move, so Diana stepped on the gas and pulled around it to the right, faster than she should have, but she was trying to make a point, and she was shaking, her heart was racing. The minivan went up over the curb, and as it did, it tipped hard to the right. Diana could feel the grass and dirt give way under her tires, and she saw a spray of it—black and green—spin into the air as she accelerated.

The girls continued to sing, and when Diana was directly beside the station wagon, she honked again and shot an angry look at the driver, who turned and looked back at Diana slowly, without expression.

It was an old woman.

She was wearing some kind of hat with long hat pins in it, and a little veil of lace, and Diana felt ashamed, driving away. The old woman looked serious, and wise, and when Diana looked back at her in the side mirror, she saw that the old woman had stepped out of the station wagon.

Why?

She was leaning on a cane and... what?

Waving?

Was she trying to call Diana back?

Did she need help?

Or was she shaking a fist in anger?

The old woman receded, with her station wagon, in the rearview mirror, but Diana could see that she was wearing a print dress and a long rope of pearls, a little fox stole around her neck, and the hat . . .

Eleanor Roosevelt.

Eleanor Roosevelt, Diana thought, though she continued to drive faster down Roosevelt Avenue, and the girls continued to sing behind her.

After school, they walk around the neighborhood.

It's one of the last warm afternoons of autumn. October. Behind the orange leaves, the tree branches are coal black. There's a smell in the air. Fermentation. A tree has dropped crab apples all over the grass, and bees are buzzing in circles around their softness. A gray-bearded professor pedals past them on a red Schwinn bike. He says nothing, but he smiles and nods at the girls, and they wave flirtatiously at him and smile back.

One of the girls says to the other, "I have to tell you something."

It startles her friend, to whom it's never before occurred there could be anything left unspoken between them. What they do is talk. They talk on the way to school, after school, and from their mothers' apartments at night on the phone. *She* has never waited to tell her friend anything. "What is it?" she asks.

The other girl breathes deeply, then says, "Nate Witt asked me out."

There are footsteps behind them, and both girls turn around fast. It's the mailman. He smiles. He's young and handsome. He looks Cuban, maybe Puerto Rican. He has curly black hair and dark eyes.

"Excuse me," he says, walking around the two girls. He smells like cigarettes and aftershave as he passes.

"His name is Randall," one of the girls tells the other.

"How do you know?"

The other girl shrugs. "I asked him once, when I was a kid," she said.

They watch him walk up the steps of a white clapboard house, the kind the girls wished they lived in—bric-a-brac, wood floors, front porch with two wicker rockers rocking emptily on it. There's a wild patch of daisies growing in the side garden, and a black butterfly rises from them and passes into the neighbor's yard.

A blond woman comes to the door just as the mailman steps onto the porch.

"Hi, Randall," she says, and takes a manila envelope from him. "Thank you."

One of the girls shakes her head, remembering what her friend has just told her.

"Nate Witt *asked you out*?" she says.

"Yeah," her friend says.

"Oh my god! When? And why didn't you tell me?" she asks, putting her hands on her hips, pretending to be angry.

"I don't know," her friend says, shrugging. "I . . . Are you jealous?" she asks.

"Hell, yes, I'm jealous," the other girl says, but there's a frenetic glow around her blond hair as if she is purely and simply happy for her friend.

The mailman walks across the lawn, stepping widely over a shallow ditch between one property and the next. He's whistling. It's a song both girls have heard on the radio, a song they've sung together.

"So where are you going with Nate Witt, *traitor*?"

DIANA GRABBED THE HANDLE TO THE BACK DOOR OF THE minivan and slid it open to let the little girls out.

They spilled from the backseat, laughing.

"Girls!" Diana shouted after them as they ran into the parking lot without bothering to check whether any cars were coming. The girls slowed down, turned around, and Emma motioned with her arm for her mother to follow, then turned and continued to run.

Diana threw her purse over her shoulder and went after them.

It was only ten o'clock in the morning but already warm. The sun had spread a deeply yellow melted light all over the entrance to the zoo. The other mothers who'd driven, along with Sister Beatrice, were there waiting at the ticket booth, looking toward Diana with what seemed to be impatience. Diana felt indignant. She'd driven there straight from Our Lady of Fatima. Except for the station wagon stopped in front of them, she'd come without delay. How had the others gotten there so much more quickly?

"Here," Sister Beatrice said handing four tickets to Diana. "These are yours."

Diana took the tickets and handed one to each of the girls, who took them and, without saying anything, slipped past their classmates and their mothers to the gate.

Diana followed.

The gate to the zoo was wrought iron and old-fashioned,

tipped with spears. As she passed through it a small ugly man stopped her by touching her arm.

"Ticket," he said.

She handed it to him, and he ripped it in half.

"Thank you," Diana said.

A loud cackling exploded from a tree near the duck pond just ahead, but when Diana looked toward the branches, she could see nothing but leaves. There was that smell—the smell of sperm—coming from those leaves, and it mingled with the other zoo smells. Sawdust. Dung. Wet feathers. Fur. It was, Diana imagined, what Earth would smell like from heaven.

"Have a good time," the ugly man said, handing the ripped half ticket back to Diana.

He sounded, perhaps, sarcastic.

Diana was barely past the entrance and had already lost track of the girls. They'd run ahead, and Diana thought she saw Emma skipping up the path to the monkey pit. She was too far away to hear her if Diana called, so Diana just hurried after.

When she was Emma's age Diana had come to this zoo with her own elementary school. She'd come on other occasions with her mother. She'd come with her father on the Saturdays she saw him when she was still very small. Once, her father had brought a girlfriend along with them to the zoo. It was a chance for the girlfriend, who could only have been about twenty-three years old, to pretend to be Diana's stepmother. Dress rehearsal. Diana let her. She held the girlfriend's hand and asked her to help put a barrette, which had fallen out, back into her hair.

The girlfriend ate it up. She bought Diana a stuffed lion cub at the zoo gift shop. She hugged and kissed Diana good-bye, as if she were already her stepmother, but Diana never saw that girlfriend again. Her father had never remarried.

And Diana had come to this zoo with boyfriends. She'd come here with Maureen. She'd come here with Paul. She'd been pregnant here. She'd pushed Emma in a stroller through this zoo...

Headed toward the monkey pit, Diana knew before she reached it exactly what the pit would look like and what the monkeys would be doing. There would be one monkey swinging from a rope between one boulder and the next. There would be a mother monkey and her baby lounging on one of those boulders. The mother would pat the baby absently when it rolled close to her, but she'd be looking at the children who were looking at her... distantly, not worried, but not apathetic either. She'd be taking it in. She'd be thinking. There would be many thoughts in her primal mind. Some curiosity. Some terror. Maybe a bit of hatred.

Diana noticed, ahead of her, that the other mothers, children, and Sister Beatrice were taking the path toward the snake house, but Diana stayed on the path to the monkey pit because she was sure she'd seen her daughter headed in that direction.

The path was sticky.

It seemed freshly tarred.

The heels of Diana's sandals stuck to it and came out snapping at her feet.

She'd worn tight jeans—too tight, she realized now. A man who was emptying garbage cans, looking in them for returnable bottles, looked at her legs and ass as she walked by. He was about forty years old and had a camera around his neck. As she passed him he made a clicking sound with his tongue, and Diana pulled her shirt (a short-sleeved top, red) further down over her stomach. It had begun to creep up her torso in her hurrying.

The man looked familiar, but she gave him a blank look.

She was growing concerned.

She'd already let the girls get away from her, and who knew which direction they'd go in after the monkey pit? It wasn't a large zoo, but it sprawled, and it could easily take a whole morning to track down the girls if they didn't stay in one place for long.

Diana started to sweat. She could feel it on the back of her neck like blood. She touched herself there, then looked at her fingertips, but there was no blood on them.

Diana exhaled in exasperation when she got to the top of the rise and saw that the girls weren't there.

The monkeys, however, were doing exactly what Diana knew they would be doing. For only a moment she paused to look into the eyes of the mother monkey, who pursed her lips and looked back.

It reminded her, absurdly, of Mrs. Mueler....

May I please look in your purse, young lady?

Or her mother...

Your friend Maureen called, her mother might have said with that very expression.

Diana nodded.

"I like Maureen," her mother said. She had a sponge in her hand and began to wipe it in circles around the Formica-topped kitchen table.

"We're going to the zoo," Diana told her.

"Now there's a wholesome way to spend a Sunday afternoon," her mother said sarcastically. "I don't suppose that was your *idea, was it?"*

"No, it was Maureen's," Diana said.

"You're not wearing that—" her mother said, nodding at Diana's T-shirt. It was black, tight, ripped.

"I'm going to wear a sweater over it," she said.

"Oh, great. Well, I hope it doesn't get hot and you have to take the

sweater off, because this hole here"—she put a finger in the ripped seam of the shirt and pulled it away from Diana's chest—"is an advertisement for something I hope you're not planning to sell."

The mother monkey smacked her lips, narrowed her eyes, shook her head...

"Emma!"

Diana yelled it loud enough that everyone within hearing range turned and looked at her—everyone except the blond girl in the pink windbreaker who might have been her daughter running far ahead up a hill toward the African safari.

Diana hurried after that flash of golden light as fast as she could without appearing, she hoped, to the other zoo goers to be a panicked woman, and as fast as she could in her flimsy sandals with their short but narrow heels.

Running, again, she had to pass the man who'd clicked his tongue at her. He was at another garbage can this time. He was fishing through it, lifting a magazine out of the debris. Diana could run only so fast, her heels catching in the sticky tar, and over his shoulder she could see what it was.

A dirty magazine. A glossy picture of a naked girl. She had blond hair, and she was leaning backward into a couch that had been draped with a black satin sheet.

"Don't I know you, baby?" he growled as she hurried past.

Breath

When she got to the place where she thought she'd seen Emma, Diana was out of breath, and the little girl she'd thought was hers had disappeared again. "Shit!" she said to herself, but out loud, then looked around to see if anyone had heard.

Sister Beatrice was standing beside her, looking as if she, too, had been running. Perhaps all this time she'd been running right behind, or directly beside, Diana.

The idea made Diana's heart race even harder.

She tried to smile at Sister Beatrice. But Sister Beatrice looked angry. Her tight cheeks were red, and her chin trembled as she spoke. She was carrying an armload of manila folders full of papers, as if she hadn't been able to bear the idea of leaving schoolwork behind in the classroom even for an afternoon, even on the last day of school.

"Is there some problem?" Sister Beatrice asked impatiently, shifting the weight of the folders and papers in her arms. "We've been trying to stay together as a group, but we couldn't find you or your girls—"

"I thought," Diana said, pointing up the path toward the lion's den, "that I saw Emma running in this direction."

"You mean you don't know where the girls *are*?" Sister Beatrice said, making no effort whatsoever to hide her exasperation.

"I know they went in this direction," Diana said, suddenly and absurdly worried that she might begin to cry, "but they got ahead of me."

Sister Beatrice looked full of energy and rage. Her face was like those Diana had seen on medieval beings—gryphons, gargoyles. It was stone gray, frozen, full of meaning.

Diana turned from Sister Beatrice's terrible gaze to the direction of the African safari, and she said, "I'll go get the girls, and we'll join you—"

"Immediately," Sister Beatrice finished the sentence for her.

A breeze stirred the nun's black robes, and they flapped around her arms like wings, even making the sound of wings beating at still air. Diana walked away from her as quickly as she could, and when she turned at the entrance to the African safari and looked back, Sister Beatrice was gone.

The winter of their senior year passes like a strange white dream...

Snow falling on snow. The sky, like a heavy gray lid over Briar Hill. Their down jackets become so much a part of them, it's how they recognize each other... one of the girls in her silver down jacket, the other in black, and Nate Witt in olive green.

The cafeteria smells like steam, pasta, boiled carrots. The three of them sit together at a table near the vending machines. One of the girls has her hand on his knee. He has his arm around her. Between bites of their lunches, they kiss.

Now it's always the three of them.

The three of them in Nate Witt's black Buick in the morning on the way to school, in the afternoon on the way home from school. The three of them in the cafeteria. The three of them on the weekends . . . at a movie, or eating pizza, or watching MTV in the living room of Nate Witt's parents' house.

For Valentine's Day he gives them both boxes of candy, and he gives one of them, the one with whom he is in love, a silver ring and a card he's made himself with *Be mine, I love you* written on it in his own sloppy hand.

The floor of the cafeteria is muddy from melted slush.

One of the girls kisses Nate Witt, slipping her arms around his waist, then running her hand over the top of his head, smoothly shaved.

The other girl sits across from them, smiling. She eats an ice-cream sandwich, which leaves chocolate cake on her fingertips.

"Yuck," her friend says. "Here, you can have my napkin."

She reaches across the table and hands her friend the napkin.

"Thanks," she says, wiping the sticky sweetness off her fingertips with the napkin given to her. Her friend kisses Nate Witt deep and long.

Family . . .

The word floats through her slowly.

All around her the student body makes a mumbled roar. They, too, are a kind of family. And the teachers, and the janitors. She sees them every day and they see her. There's a something that rises from them and buzzes around the fluorescent lights—although they've all been together so long they no longer hear the background noise of their strange love for one another. Just once in a while, when it surges, or when it's cut through with sudden hate....

A FEW KITSCHY THINGS HAD BEEN ADDED TO THE AFRICAN safari since Diana had last been there.

Some plaster palm trees with some plaster natives under them, painted a deep and shining black and carrying spears...

An old jeep with two dummies in it—a white man and woman wearing khaki vests and shorts and big wide-brimmed hats.

Diana hurried past them, but not before she passed close enough to the jeep to see the man behind the wheel. He was staring straight ahead, hands on the steering wheel, with an expression of total absence. He must have been, once, a department store mannequin—he had the Ken-doll features for it—and been retired to the zoo. The sun was shining brightly through the windshield into his eyes, but he didn't blink.

"Diana."

She turned around fast, but there was no one.

It had been a man's voice... a familiar voice.

Paul?

But behind her there was nothing except the path leading out of the African safari, past the jeep and the natives staring into the future blankly, their painted skin glistening as if with sweat. Ahead of her was a flight of stairs that led up a small hill, where Diana knew the lions were—but there was no one, either, on those stairs.

"Diana."

This time she jumped when she heard it. She turned around fast and put a hand to her forehead to block the sun from her eyes, which stung. Her heart was beating hard. She was scared, though she didn't know why...

Scared that the dummy would speak to her from the jeep?

Or one of the natives?

She considered, briefly, running in the direction of the lions, when she saw him standing in the shade of the plaster palm trees.

Could it be?

Diana took a step closer. She squinted and blinked and saw that it was.

"Mr. McCleod?" she said.

"Yes," he said, nodding.

Diana laughed out loud and took a few quick steps toward him.

"I can't believe it!" she said.

"Did you think I would be dead?" he asked. It had to have been a joke, but he sounded serious.

"No," Diana said, laughing and shaking her head. "Of course not. It's just... been so long!"

Mr. McCleod took a step toward her and out of the shade, into the sun, where she could see him better. He looked old....

Ancient.

The skin on his face and hands was covered with dark spots, and he was stooped, leaning on a cane.

But of course. How old must he have been by now? And still he looked like Mr. McCleod. He was wearing a short-sleeved yellow shirt, and there were pens in his pockets. He'd grown sideburns, which struck Diana as odd. It seemed like the kind of thing a man would have had when he was young, then abandoned when he got older, instead of the other way around.

Diana reached out her hand, and he put his in hers. It felt light but warm. She squeezed it, and Mr. McCleod smiled, but he also pulled the hand away from hers quickly as if she'd been a bit too forward, as if he weren't merely shy but was trying to let her know that her squeeze had been inappropriate.

Diana felt herself blush.

Mr. McCleod said, "You're looking well."

"Thank you," she said. "So are you. I—I can't believe you would remember me, you had so many students."

"How could I forget you?" Mr. McCleod asked. "You were our Mayqueen."

"Oh," Diana said, touching her neck and feeling the blood beating faster under the thin skin there. Mayqueen...

She'd almost forgotten.

"Are you still teaching?" she asked him.

Mr. McCleod snorted. "Of course not. I retired years ago—"

"Oh," Diana said, embarrassed. "I wouldn't have guessed—"

"That I was so old?"

"No," Diana said quickly, perhaps too brightly. "You just seemed to love teaching so much that—"

Again Mr. McCleod snorted.

"Jim!" a voice called from behind Diana, who turned to see a large old woman hobbling down the steps from the lion's den. She was gesturing (angrily?) at Mr. McCleod. Diana had never known his name was Jim... or if she had she'd long since forgotten.

"Jim!" the old woman shouted again and made a swooping gesture with her arm, calling Mr. McCleod to her.

"You'll have to excuse me," he said to Diana. "I have to go."

"Of course," Diana said. "I'm so glad I saw you. I always remember—"

Again Mr. McCleod snorted. It was dismissive and, Diana thought, full of contempt. She'd been about to tell him that she'd never forgotten his telling them that the brain contained more nerve cells than the universe contained stars. She'd always, after learning that simple fact in Mr. McCleod's biology class, thought of her mind as a darkness full of stars.

She'd been listening, she wanted him to know.

She'd understood what he was trying to impress them with—the enormity, the complexity, of *themselves.* Even today she could have mapped the parts of the brain if he'd given her the quiz: *Medulla, hypothalamus, corpus callosum, cerebellum*...

Mr. McCleod didn't say good-bye. He and the old woman climbed the stairs to the lion's den together, and Diana watched them go. It had been the direction she'd planned to go in, but now she thought she'd wait until they were well ahead of her, until they had gone far enough that she wouldn't run into them again.

Nate Witt has left to visit his grandmother for the weekend.

So, even though it's Friday afternoon, the girls are alone together. They're eating microwave popcorn and drinking diet Coke. One of their mothers comes home and tosses her black shoulder bag onto the couch, kicks off her flat shoes.

"Hi, Deb," one of the girls says, the one who isn't her daughter.

There's nothing to call one another's mothers except their first names. Both of them had changed back to their maiden names when they'd divorced, so they have different names than their daughters. It's impossible to remember those names, or to know whether to call someone's divorced mother *Mrs?... Miss?... Ms?*

"Hi, Mom," the other girls says.

Her mother pulls out one of the kitchen table chairs and sits down with the girls. She takes a handful of popcorn out of the Tupperware bowl and inhales. She says, "I'm taking you two girls to a lecture tonight. It'll be good for you."

The girls look at each other, each one makes an expression of fake horror.

"A *lecture*?" one of them asks, leaving her mouth open for emphasis.

"A lecture," her mother says. "Like I said, it'll be good for you. Maybe you'll learn something."

"I don't want to learn something. It's Friday night. We're going—"

"Come on," her mother says. "Please? This professor in our department has been asked to give this lecture, and it's a big deal, and I have to go, and he's a nice man, who— He's brilliant, really. And cute."

"I'll go," says the one who's not her daughter, the one who can think of nothing she'd want to do tonight without Nate Witt, anyway.

Her friend gives her a dirty look. "Thanks a lot, girlfriend," she says.

DIANA FOLLOWED AN ARROW THAT SAID *ELLA THE ELEPHANT,* thinking she'd turn back toward the lion's den after she'd given Mr. McCleod and the old woman a good head start.

The path to Ella the elephant was scattered with peanut shells. A bit more kitsch. Diana imagined someone out there every morning emptying a bag of empty shells onto the dirt.

The sign and the path and the elephant were new since Diana had last been to the zoo. For decades there'd been no elephant at Briar Hill Park and Zoo, not since Diana had been a child. *That* elephant had also been named Ella, and she'd died under mysterious circumstances. One summer afternoon she'd simply collapsed under her own enormous weight, having never displayed a single symptom of disease.

Articles were written about Ella in the newspaper. There were photographs of her, dead, on the front page for days. Her legs and trunk were under her body, and she'd had her forehead pressed to the ground. She looked as if she'd fallen out of the sky.

Why had she died?

An investigation was ordered. The government got involved. Elephant experts were flown in from all over the world to study Ella's terrible carcass.

Not a heart attack. Not a blood clot. Poisoning was suspected.

But who would have poisoned the elephant?

Someone who worked at the zoo?

Someone who visited the zoo?

A rumor sprang up that *children—teenagers*—had poisoned Ella, and whether there was any truth to it or not, Diana never knew, having been only nine or ten years old at the time. But the idea of it caught fire in Briar Hill, and the town, as if to punish its young, refused to replace the elephant. The signs pointing the way to the elephant pit were taken down, and that part of the zoo was closed off completely.

But now the elephant apparently was back. Diana could smell her. A sweetly acidic smell mixed with wet straw, foliage, shit. And she could feel the dirt path vibrate through the flimsy soles of her sandals, as if kettle drums were being played underground.

The elephant was stomping in the pit.

They'd planted tropical trees along the edge of the path since Diana had last walked it (how did they manage it in this climate?), and the leaves made a lush tunnel that bent lower and lower over the path until Diana could feel the fronds brushing the top of her head as she hurried along. A thick humidity was rising from the earth beneath the peanut shells, and there was a small swarm—a small gray cloud, like a brain—of gnats hovering in midair along the path.

Diana had to run through them with her hands covering her eyes.

When she was through the cloud and had uncovered her eyes, Ella was closer than she'd expected. She hadn't even planned to see the elephant. She'd wanted simply to walk to the end of the path, then hurry back toward the lion's den.

But there Ella was, only a few feet away from Diana, alone in the elephant pit.

She was standing in a shallow puddle of urine, and there was a steel ring around one of her ankles. A rusty chain was attached to one end of the ring, and the other end was attached to a steel post.

Diana stood sweating and still at the end of the tropical tunnel from which she'd emerged more quickly than she'd expected, staring at Ella.

Ella stared back.

Diana could still feel the earth vibrating dully under her feet, but the elephant *wasn't* stomping. The elephant was only standing, looking as though she hadn't moved in years.

Ella blinked, then turned her face away from Diana, then swooped her huge head back to look at Diana again.

There was no one else around.

Diana felt ashamed and as though she ought to speak if she were going to stand there and stare. . . .

Ella's eyes were enormous, and glassy, and as full of suffering and hope as anything Diana had ever seen.

Diana cleared her throat. With no one but Ella to hear, what difference did it make if she spoke?

Ella shifted a bit, and the chain at her ankle scraped against the cement floor of the elephant pit.

Diana took a step forward and said, "How could I have forgotten you?"

RUMBLING

HER DAUGHTER . . .

Diana had almost forgotten what she was doing, why she was at the zoo. She took a last look at Ella, who didn't move and didn't blink, whose eyes were full of loneliness and longing. Still, that vibration under the ground.

Diana lifted her hand to say good-bye, then turned and hurried back toward the jungle tunnel that had led her there.

When she was beneath the greenness of it again, the rumbling became even louder, and Diana stopped for a moment and turned to look back toward the pit, to the place from which the rumbling seemed to come.

It had to be some kind of underground machine. A generator that powered the whole zoo. Some kind of enormous furnace being stoked. Ella was still watching her, still hadn't moved—but coming from her direction, there was the sound of a *herd* of elephants running through a jungle.

Neither girl has ever been to a lecture.

It takes place in the auditorium on campus where they were each taken, as little girls, to see the Nutcracker ballet.

The carpet is a rich aqua blue, and the ceiling above them is inlaid with gold. They sit with one of the girl's mothers, in a row not far from the front, a row of seats that has been roped off for those who work in the philosophy department.

The heavy velvet curtains have already been opened, revealing a stage with nothing but a podium on it. Beside the podium there is a small table with a pitcher of water and a single glass.

Tonight the auditorium is completely full. People who've come to hear the lecture have to stand along the walls because there are no seats left. The mumbling of the audience sounds like locomotion. It doesn't grow louder or quieter until the lights flash—off, on—and then the whole auditorium goes suddenly and obediently silent.

When Professor McFee steps out on the stage, there's immediate applause.

The applause goes on and on.

The professor looks happy but embarrassed. He nods into the applause as if it were a wind. He glances into the audience nervously.

He isn't a young man, but he has a child's eyes—darting and bright blue. He's wearing a suit, but it looks a bit rumpled, uncomfortable, as if it's hung in a closet for many years without being worn. He has a neatly trimmed beard and mustache with just a touch of gray.

When he puts the folder he's carrying onto the podium, the audience quits clapping, but there's still a feeling in the air like applause—goodwill, appreciation—before he has even spoken.

Professor McFee at the podium looks up, nervous, and says, "It's one of the greatest honors of my life to have been asked to give the Arthur M. Fuller lecture this year."

One of the girls—the one who wanted to come to the lecture in the first place—looks at the other and rolls her eyes.

But the other looks away from her, back to the man on the stage.

He begins by clearing his throat, looking down at his notes, then up at the audience, and then he says, "Many have asked the question Why is there evil? The question *I* want to ask tonight is, Why is there *good*?"

For the two hours of his lecture, one of the girls never again takes her eyes from the reddish light around this man, whose humility and brightness are greater than anything she's ever seen. Until this moment she didn't know such men existed in the world.

Professor McFee talks about good and evil as if he has thought a lot about them, as if he has spent a *lifetime* thinking about them, reading about them, wondering...

"Why," he asks, "are human beings capable, as no other animals seem to be, of *intentional evil*? Can it be so that human beings will therefore also be capable of *intentional good*?

"If evil exists, as the Old Testament implies that it does, to test and strengthen the virtue of the good, to what high angel may we turn for guidance when faced with a choice for evil or good?"

A long pause.

"To the *conscience,*" he answers his own question, "which is the mirror that can't be tarnished but must be located. *Conscience is the voice of God in the nature and heart of man . . .*"

One of the girls takes a pen and a piece of paper out of her purse and writes that down.

SHE BEGAN TO RUN . . .

Out of the jungle tunnel littered with peanut shells and back into the clearing where she'd seen Mr. McCleod. Now there was no one there. Just the jeep with its blank-eyed driver and his female companion leaning awkwardly away from him as if she'd been jostled on a bumpy road and never propped back up.

And the natives, who didn't bother to look at her.

Diana ran toward the steps that led up to the lion's den, stumbling in her sandals, out of breath.

What if her daughter wasn't there?

She looked at her wrist, but she hadn't put her watch on this morning. Instead she had an armful of useless silver bracelets. What time could it have been? How long had she stopped to talk to Mr. McCleod? How long had she stood looking at Ella, the elephant? She looked at the sky, and the sun was directly in the center of it—noon—but could it have been only noon?

Of course . . .

Of course it was only noon.

The sun couldn't just stop like a dead watch in the sky.

It was only noon. They had *hours* until they were supposed to meet again at the entrance of the zoo.

But Diana continued hurrying up the stairs to the lion's den, feeling weak with breathlessness. Hot and tired. The glare of the summer sun on the tropical leaves of the African safari seemed so bright—brighter than the sun itself—that Diana could hardly see. And there was a high whining coming from somewhere over her head and in her inner ear at the same time. She put her hand to her temple as she hurried up the stairs and tried to stop the pain there before it started, but when she did this she dropped her purse.

It fell tumbling behind her down the stairs, and Diana turned and watched it tumble, hoping it wouldn't spill...

But it did.

She saw her wallet fall out, a small shower of silver and copper coins, and then a tampon, and then—though she knew it couldn't have been—a clear plastic Baggie of marijuana.

It was wrapped up tightly with a rubber band, but even from where she was standing many steps above it, Diana could see the crushed, illegal leaves of it gleaming darkly in the sun.

"Mrs. McFee?"

Diana turned around fast to see Sister Beatrice standing above her, a black silhouette with wings. She could only blink up at her, because the sun shining behind Sister Beatrice was so brilliant and her dark robes only barely blocked it out. She was still carrying her load of manila folders and notebooks. They looked disorganized, unwieldy, as if they'd been dropped and picked back up and insufficiently reorganized.

"Oh," Diana said. "I—" She pointed to the stairs that rose behind Sister Beatrice in dusty stations. "I was just on my way... there... to find the girls."

"You dropped your purse," Sister Beatrice said.

"I know," Diana said, and smiled weakly. She felt afraid to move, to hurry toward the Baggie of marijuana, which would have been an admission of guilt.

But it wasn't hers.

It hadn't been hers for more than *two decades*...

How—?

Sister Beatrice was looking at it. There was a tension around her eyes. A recognition.

"I found your girls," Sister Beatrice said. "They're not at the lion's den anymore. They've gone to look at the wolves."

Sister Beatrice pointed to the path that led back out of the African safari, and when she did, the manila folders in her arms shifted and a few papers flew loose from her grasp. They floated downward on the breeze, landing on the stairs at Diana's feet.

Diana bent over and picked them up, brushed a bit of dirt off of them, and then she put them neatly together and held them up to Sister Beatrice. "Here you go," Diana said, trying to sound helpful, obedient, a good student.

The nun reached out to take them quickly, but before she could snatch the papers out of Diana's hand, Diana saw the paper that was on top.

It had been folded into fourths, then very carefully smoothed flat again.

The large bold type was in a familiar font. Her daughter's name was written in blue pen in her daughter's familiar writing in the upper right-hand corner of the page.

> *Bethany Maria Anna Elizabeth was an orphan in a convent until I adopted her. Her favorite food is Froot Loops. Bethany Maria Anna Elizabeth does not like math tests or science as much as she likes ice cream! When she grows up she wants to be a mommy.*

"Give me that," Sister Beatrice snapped.

"But," Diana blurted, trying to hold on to the piece of paper, "it's Emma's story, the one—"

Sister Beatrice managed to snatch the piece of paper out of Diana's hand, and when she had it again she stuffed it among the manila folders and other papers. Diana saw it disappear and knew she'd never get it back again. She looked up. Now she was only a foot or two away from Sister Beatrice's face, and she could see how angry the nun was. Her jaw was clenched. Her eyes were narrowed, as if she were about to make a threat.

"It was you," Diana said. A realization, but it wasn't an accusation. She was simply understanding something aloud and for the first time. "You changed Emma's story?" She looked up at Sister Beatrice, full of wonder.

"Oh, *shut up,*" Sister Beatrice said. She walked stiffly past Diana on the stairs. She hadn't said it loudly but had said it with such force that Diana felt, briefly, that it might have struck her dumb, that it might have been a curse, that she might never speak again.

But then Sister Beatrice's black robes brushed her arm, and Diana could feel her hot breath close to her cheek. It stank... her breath. It smelled as if something had rotted in her mouth.

"Why?" Diana asked her as she passed.

Sister Beatrice turned and looked straight into Diana's eyes, then smiled.

The smile was full of hate.

"Because I don't like you," Sister Beatrice said.

She stepped over the contents of Diana's spilled purse... the coins, the tampon, the Baggie of marijuana.

"Why?" Diana asked.

But the nun kept walking. She reached the bottom of the stairs and began to walk faster, and from where Diana watched her, Sister Beatrice in her black habit looked like the shadow of a crow flying overhead, or a small and awful angel...

The avenging angel, the accusing angel, the angel who did not forget, who did not forgive, its shadow circling the world endlessly.

It's Saturday. . . .

Nate Witt is at his job at Uncle Ed's Oil Change, so the girls are together without him for the afternoon. It's the end of April and everything has begun to melt. The smell of rot and fresh growth is in the air. The green swords of tulips and daffodils have made their way out of the earth.

The girls notice these as they go for their first walk through the neighborhood after so much winter. They're wearing tight jeans, black boots, short-sleeved shirts, and they've tied sweaters around their waists. One of the girls is wearing a silver ring that was given to her by Nate.

"I think you're going to be elected Mayqueen," she says to her friend.

"No fucking way," the other says. "It's you or Melissa Maroney, but I think it will be you—"

"Why me?"

"Because you're beautiful—"

"Not as beautiful as you." She means it. It's easy to say.

"Yeah, you are," her friend says, and nudges her with her shoulder. "Plus, I've got a reputation. No one gets elected Mayqueen at Briar Hill who's—"

"Well, it won't be me. Not now that I'm dating Nate. He's—"

"Oh, everybody loves it that you're with Nate. The born-again Christian and the biker boy."

The dark-haired girl laughs. "I don't know. Maybe. Probably Melissa."

"No," the other says. "Melissa's too *out there.* Mayqueen is usually some girl who's kept to herself... a bit of a mystery... not such a social butterfly."

"Well, I don't want to be Mayqueen."

It's a lie, and not.

They turn the corner near the Catholic girls' school. Our Lady of Fatima. It sits at the top of a hill. They've walked past it a million times on their way to other places. Sometimes the school yard is full of little girls in white blouses and plaid skirts.

One of the girls gasps.

At first she gasps because of what she thinks she's seen. Hundreds of little girls in stiff white blouses, but when she realizes it's something else, at first she thinks she's dreaming. The whole surface of the green hill is fluttering with something. It's dazzling, cumulative.

"What the hell?" she says, looking harder.

"Little crosses," the other explains.

"Why?"

"The unborn," the other tells her. "I saw the little girls putting out the crosses yesterday. And the pro-lifers..."

The other girl walks in the direction of the crosses. She's seen pictures of Arlington Cemetery, and it's like that—seeing that strange quiet from the sky—row after row of stiff white arms embracing the air, the emptiness and shadows.

There are hundreds—*thousands*?—of these small white crosses covering every inch of the hill. Plastic. White. Some have fallen over into the green grass, but most have been planted deeply enough in the ground that they're fluttering only a little in the breeze.

"Come on, let's go," her friend says, taking her elbow.

But her friend stands, still staring.

They're like a dream against the green. Stunning in their uniformity. The absolute conviction of their posture.

"Jesus," she says. "It's—"

"It's a statement, that's for sure," the other girl says.

And then the other girl notices that there's a name on every cross, on every one of the hundreds and hundreds of small white crosses on the elementary school lawn.

She bends down to look at one which is only a few inches from the toes of her black boot.

In a child's cursive, with a black Magic Marker, *Emma* is written there.

DIANA SAW HER DAUGHTER FROM A DISTANCE AND recognized her instantly. She was standing alone looking into the bars of a cage, her pink windbreaker tied around her waist.

"Emma!"

But Emma didn't turn to look. Either she hadn't heard her mother calling her or she'd chosen not to answer.

Diana began to run.

This part of the zoo was called the Black Forest. It was landscaped with pine trees and rocks, and a small waterfall that made the sound of mechanical splashing into a cement basin. There were fairy-tale characters, plaster statues painted brightly but amateurishly here and there—a woodcutter, a witch with a gingerbread house, ogres and dwarves, Rapunzel with ropes of golden hair, Sleeping Beauty laid out on what appeared to be a stretcher, with her eyes closed, surrounded by tangled briars—and the paths were scattered with redwood chips. The smell of forest and water was dank and dry at the same time.

Inside the cages there were dens for coyotes, foxes, wolves, and although Diana couldn't see them, she could sense their eyes watching her from the darkness. If there was an owl in the owl cage, it was standing so still she couldn't see it.

"Emma!" she called again.

This time Emma looked up. "Mommy," she said, but didn't move.

"Mommy," she said again, and pointed to a place just beyond the wolf's cage, where the wolf was. . . .

"You're not going to believe it," one of the girls says to the other.

It's the end of April, and the cafeteria is humid with rain. Nate Witt has his arm around her. "I was elected Mayqueen. Mr. McCleod just told me."

The other girl stands up and puts her arm around her friend, who smells like chocolate milk and flesh. She presses her face into her friend's dark hair—her friend.

There's April in her hair. Motion and stillness. Wings and earth. There are tears, and there is . . . *friendship.* There is velvet, and traveling, and distance, bones and blood, summer coming again as it always does, *love.*

"Are you jealous?" her friend asks.

"Hell, yes," she says. But everything is inside her as she holds her friend, her *best friend,* in this embrace. . . .

Tomorrow. Last year. Her own daughter. Her mother, and *her* mother . . .

Life seems suddenly—in the general din of the world and the cafeteria, in the last months of her senior year—very short and also very long. Eternal.

All of it is inside her.

Her friend is smiling. Her friend's boyfriend is also smiling. They are both inside of her... *family*... where everything else is and will always be. There's a place for both of them—just as there's a place for her heart, for her lungs. She can feel all of it inside her, *all* of it. Except for jealousy.

Where *jealousy* would be, there's nothing.

"Come on," her friend says. "If you're going to cry because I got elected Mayqueen, let's go to the girls' room, at least."

DIANA LOOKED IN THE DIRECTION OF THE WOLF'S CAGE, but it was empty. There was nothing other than a shadow moving around inside it, slipping between rocks, like the shadow of water.

Her breath was sharp in her lungs, she'd been running for so long...

When she finally reached her daughter's side, Diana sank to her knees and pulled her to her, smelled her golden hair, the side of her neck deeply, taking it in as if to memorize it—the crushed leaves and flour of her daughter, the whole melody of the baking aisle, the smell of the physical world and what was just beyond it, made of mercy and childhood and love—before she looked again in the direction of the shadow Emma was still watching with her wide blue eyes.

The shadow was moving around inside the cage, but the wolf was outside of it.

April

They're in the girl's room when they hear the first *dot-dot-dot* of semi-automatic gunfire.

It sounds phony and far away, and they keep doing what they're doing—brushing their hair, looking at their reflections in the girls'-room mirror…

Dot-dot-dot.

Dot. Dot. Dot.

"Want a LifeSaver?" one of the girls asks the other, then hands her the roll.

Her friend takes a piece of the chalk-white peppermint candy and puts it in her mouth. It tastes so clean it nearly takes her breath away.

Dot. Dot. Dot.

"What is that?" one of the girls asks the other. She stuffs

her hairbrush back into her backpack next to her anthology of English literature. She was supposed to have read the first chapter of *Daisy Miller* for a quiz that afternoon, but she hadn't even started.

Knock-knock-knock-knock-knock . . .

This time it's followed by a soft and gurgling scream.

"Shit," one of the girls says.

"What the hell—"

One of the girls starts toward the door, but the other grabs her elbow. "Don't go," she says. "What if?—"

"What?"

"I don't know." She drops her friend's elbow.

"It's just a prank. It's probably Ryan Asswipe . . ."

Dot. Dot—

THE WOLF WAS PACING OUTSIDE THE OPEN DOOR OF THE cage, looking confused, as if someone had just opened it, just let him out at that moment, as if for the first time in his life he'd found himself on the other side.

Diana screamed, and when the wolf heard it, he looked up, sniffing at the air, then turned to look behind him, as if at his own shadow, which seemed to startle him, and he began to growl.

Low at first, like a tape recording starting slow, then speeding up, and then faster and louder. It was impossible to tell whether the growling came from the world or from the shadow—or, it struck Diana as completely possible, that the growling came from inside herself. . . .

Emma didn't move.

She didn't seem to be breathing, though her nostrils were flared and there were tears in her eyes.

They never hear the door to the girls' room open.

They never hear his footsteps.

One of them is whispering the Lord's Prayer . . . *forgive us our trespasses as we forgive those* . . . when the other says under her breath, "Maybe he's gone. Maybe we ought to go for help."

The other nods yes, then opens her eyes. She opens them slowly, looking up first, then down at the linoleum floor and the space between the floor and the stall door, and then she cries out.

It's so brilliant, that cry, that the other girl looks down at her hands and sees her life like a small marble roll out of them, under the stall door, past the shoes Michael Patrick's wearing—white Nikes with blue lightning bolts on the sides, laces untied—too far and too quick to get it back.

THE WOLF BARED HIS TEETH.

He was about twelve feet away, but Diana could see and smell him. He was a wild animal. No one's pet. She'd seen him before—the blue eyes, the howling in the next room—but that was something else, that was before he became this, before he began this life.

His teeth were white. His gums were pink. But he'd never been bathed except by the rain that fell on his cage. He'd lived his whole life in that cage. He smelled like salt and breath, and his fur was matted, especially on his back. There was blood on the fur on his face. He lifted up his muzzle and sniffed the air, sniffing them—then took, in their direction, one slow gray step, then crouched.

"So," he says too loudly, and both girls flinch...

"So," he says more softly, as if sorry to have startled them. "Which one of you girls should I kill?"

"MOMMY," EMMA SAID AGAIN, AND THEN SHE WHIMPERED.

And it was the sound of her daughter's voice that woke Diana up to herself.

"Mommy..."

For a second Diana could actually see the light from the sun pouring itself into the air, floating in front of her in fluid strands, weightless as hair.

This was the moment she'd been born for. The moment she'd been allowed to grow into the martyrdom of middle age for, and become a mother. The moment in which she gave up *herself—the bells and the bracelets, and the pyramids and planets, all the things of the world she'd seen and never see...*

One of the girls swallows. "Please," she whispers, "don't kill either of us."

She keeps her eyes open. For a moment, she smells her dog, Muppet. Muppet just in from the rain, quivering against her chest like a muscle made of affection.

Michael Patrick smiles.

"Oh, but I'm going to kill one of you," he says, "so which one should it be?"

The other girl sobs. It's warm, and full of water. She remembers Mr. McCleod telling the class that the heart is 95 percent water and that the brain...

She can't remember, but she knows it's water, too. Warm water. Salty water. The mind, the soul, memory... all of it floating in that water. Time, and love, and terror, swimming through a body made mostly out of tears.

She swallows the tears, closes her eyes, sees her mother standing in the doorway, wearing a white nightgown. Her mother's eyes are wide. Her face is creased from sleep. She's half awake but ready to run through the doorway, to shake her daughter awake, calling out her name. Then she sees her father at Circuit City selling a stereo to a student. (Briefly, without knowing why, he thinks of her.)

Behind Michael Patrick the mirror, which the two girls only moments ago stepped out of, shines clean and empty, except for his back reflected in it.

All these years, they both marvel, they'd never even really noticed him—an ugliness moving among them. A darkness opening doors, locking his bike to the bike rack, wearing a backpack full of more darkness, closing his spiral notebook on the words inside it.

All those years, that ugliness hadn't even touched them, hadn't changed them, hadn't hurt them, hadn't even occurred to them until now.

That's the real surprise, one of the girls would say to the other if she could speak to her now, if she could call her best friend on the telephone from her bedroom, if she could lean over and turn the radio down as they drove together into the weedy green of June, and say something, anything.

If she could glance at her friend's reflection beside her in the girls'-room mirror, put down her hairbrush, and smile, she'd say, *That's the miracle... the real miracle... all the goodness all our lives....*

Then one of the girls says it in a whisper. He doesn't hear her at first. He leans closer. "What?" he asks. "What did you say?"

She clears her throat and says it louder, voice shaking, but very clear, "If you're going to kill one of us, kill me.

"Kill me," she says, "not her."

"EMMA," DIANA WHISPERED INTO HER EAR, "TURN around, Emma, and run."

Again, the growling, but when Diana looked back, the place where Emma had been standing was empty. Nothing but shining, a perfect space scissored out of the air, a freedom full of little stars and powdered sugar and forgiveness and affection.

Then Michael Patrick says in a softer voice, almost as if he's sorry to have to ask, but having to ask, "And what do you have to say?"

The blond girl bows her head.

Of course. Of course he would want to know. And now, she realizes for the first time, she has never really been afraid—never, not even once before in her whole life...

This is what it is to be afraid:

The skeleton and the muscles and the blood pumping through her heart, willing her to live... all that water, trying to stay afloat in all that water.

No jealousy. No hatred, no anger, no spite or resentment. Nothing...

Just this terror, which is everything.

Michael Patrick puts the gun nearer to her ear. It touches her temple, and its blue blackness is a terrible, intimate whisper. She has to answer it. She opens her eyes and sees how empty the mirror on the girls'-room wall is except for Michael Patrick's shoulders. Still, in it she can see herself twenty years from now, driving a silver minivan into middle age, with a daughter strapped into the seat beside her. On the bumper of that minivan as it drives away, she sees a sticker. It says, CHOOSE LIFE. There will be no punishment for choosing to live, her terror tells her, except to live with this.

"Kill her," she says, "not me."

WHEN DIANA GLANCED BEHIND HER, JUST BEFORE THE darkness separated them, she cried out with joy to see her daughter darting into a row of pine trees...

Running into the fairy-tale distance, running as fast as her little legs could carry her, not looking back, not slowing down for a moment, making it safely to the other side.

And when the wolf sprang in her direction, Diana spread her arms wide to take him in.

The first shot causes a warm rain to fall on Diana's arms from the sky. The second plants a mirrored jewel in the left temporal lobe of her brain... a place she could have named on a quiz but which now seems to be the place where the future is imagined, the place where what would have been *is*.

EPILOGUE

May

Diana was Mayqueen. The whole hospital hummed like a white gown around her. An air conditioner rattled near the windows, which were blank and brilliant. Someone had wrapped her face in light to keep the darkness from draining out of her into the world. They were saying her name in whispers and screams—

Diana.

Diana.

Do you know your name?

Do you know where you are?

A man was pounding on her chest. A woman breathed into her mouth. Something was poured into her eyes, and then the eyes were taped shut, and Diana was taken away on a stretcher, which seemed to her to be circled by birds—one of every kind of bird she'd ever known in the world.

Sparrows, seagulls, robins, doves. She could have touched them, but her hands were tied. She could have named them, but she'd forgotten about words.

They flew up like dreams, then wafted away.

She's dead, someone said.

"Who? Who?" she asked.

Not you, sweetheart, he said.

She was raised, sung to, carried. A crowd gathered to watch, and then a door slammed shut behind her, and then it began...

The decades of dreaming.

The centuries and lifetimes of mirrors and dreaming.

Someone put a jar of lilacs on the tray beside her bed.

A black crow landed on the windowsill calling, *You, you,* staring into the glass, in her black habit, angry.

But Diana stared straight at her, and the bird rose, beating into the blue, and disappeared.

Machines breathed for her. There were songs. A radio. *Sweetheart, sweetheart.* She could hear her mother sobbing somewhere beyond her.

Was she being born? Born again? *She can't hear you,* she heard her father say.

But she could.

And she could see them. She could see them where they sat together in the bleachers full of grief and love. Were they even holding hands?

When Mr. McCleod settled the crown on her head, there was a tear like a tiny rhinestone in the corner of his right eye.

"You're the most beautiful Mayqueen Briar Hill High has ever had," he said.

And then the float full of real and paper roses began to shiver, and to move.

It was pulled by a long white limousine, out of the football stadium and into the high school parking lot and onto the streets of her hometown, which were lined up with people holding bouquets and chanting her name.

Diana. Diana.

Before she was pulled out of their sight, Diana turned to wave to her parents... *Good-bye, good-bye.* They were mouthing the words to her, throwing kisses in her direction, holding tightly to one another as they must have done when she was made.

She could hear music—flutes and trumpets and violins—being played for her somewhere, somewhere ahead of her, rising from the whole town, the whole world, wrapping it in clear weather. It was, after all, spring, and the breath that rose from the world was made of flowers. The street was scattered with petals.

There were so many people lining the street!

They were waving and crying and laughing as she passed.

She saw Mrs. Mueler, who was holding the red suede purse that belonged to Diana, and a ring of keys. She was smiling. She was sorry. Was she trying to hand the purse to Diana?

Diana leaned over, but the purse and the keys were out of her reach. She just laughed, and Mrs. Mueler laughed, waving... *Later, later...*

Diana saw, in the crowd, a little girl she'd known in elementary school... a chubby little blond with glasses, a girl Diana had once watched fall to her knees on the concrete steps outside their school and hadn't bothered to stop to help. The girl had cried out, and her glasses had broken, and there was blood on her face, but Diana had just kept running.

Now that girl was skipping, smiling. She was happy to see Diana. She forgave her. She was fine. She would never fall again, her smiling and waving seemed to say.

Then, over the shining heads of children—little girls holding small white crosses, wearing clean uniforms and bright pigtails—Diana saw Miss Zena in a black leotard. She had Diana's toe shoes, pink satin and ribbons, and she was running gracefully behind the crowd, mouthing Diana's name. Miss Zena whirled the toe shoes by the ribbons like a lasso in the air, then threw them over the heads of the little girls, and they flashed toward Diana and landed at her feet. Diana could see that Miss Zena was laughing and crying at the same time, and Diana waved to her as she passed, *Thank you, thank you...*

As the float turned the corner, passing the Burger King, a boy with one arm sprinted across the parking lot, holding up a bouquet of bloodred roses. He ran fast. He caught up with the float and reached up to Diana with his one arm, holding the flowers for her, and Diana was able to take them from him—and he stopped running but waved his hand wildly in the air, growing smaller and smaller as Diana passed into the crowd and the float turned the corner onto Maiden Lane. She glanced behind her then and saw a man with a gray beard and wire-rimmed glasses pedaling a red bike furiously behind the float. Professor McFee. He was crying, out of breath. He couldn't catch up. He had something to say. Something about good, about evil, about *her*. He, too, was carrying a bouquet of red roses.

Then the long white limousine that pulled the float she was riding on sped up and the houses on Maiden Lane began to flash by her faster, but Diana caught a glimpse of a little girl on the front porch of a pretty clapboard house. She was sitting in a white wicker rocker and *Timmy* was in her lap!

He was sleeping. The little girl was happy. The daisies off the side of the porch, growing wildly in their sunny spot, were harmless and full of joy. The little girl didn't wave, but when the float passed by, she looked up.

Randall, the mailman, turned on the front steps and smiled.

The float turned the corner at the apartment building where Diana lived with her mother. There she saw the blurred image of Sandy Ellsworth standing in a bikini near the curb, dragging on a joint, and Diana shook her head and couldn't help but laugh . . .

And then the long white limousine began to pull her even

faster, past the town and the houses and the apartment buildings and the churches and the schools.

Everything was in bloom.

The whole world was an arrow of beauty.

Birds zipped by her in the air. Squirrels dashed under the tires of the float, then hurried safely to the other side of the road and into the branches of the waiting trees, which bowed lower and lower in their greenness, hunching over the road, making a small dark tunnel around the float, like hands folded in a prayer, through which Diana passed.

Lilac, sparrow, sunlight, dust...

"Look," she heard her mother say.

And then the float stopped at the end of the leafy tunnel, and Diana stepped down slowly from its roses, wearing her white gown, and looked.

I would like to thank Ann Patty, Lisa Bankoff,
Bill Abernethy, and Antonya Nelson for the friendship
and assistance that made the novel possible.